EMMA WHITEHALL is an author, bookseller, editor and introvert from the North East of England.

Her work has been published in anthologies and magazines in the UK, USA, Ireland and Mexico, and she has performed her stories in various pubs, cafes, radio channels and heritage centres in the North East. A former Waterstones bookseller turned indie bookshop champion, Emma writes fun, emotion driven fantasy, with characters that you'll want to take for a coffee. Or wrap in a blanket. Or both. Emma lives in Tyne & Wear with her cat and an ever-growing to read pile.

You can find Emma at emmawhitehallwrites.squarespace.com, or on Instagram and Twitter at @pensandpizza.

D1740393

CLOCKWORK MAGPIES

EMMA WHITEHALL

Welcome to
Loxport!

NORTHODOX PRESS

Northodox Press Ltd
Maiden Greve, Malton,
North Yorkshire, YO17 7BE

This edition 2022

1

First published in Great Britain
by Northodox Press Ltd 2022

ISBN: 978-1-8383430-7-1

This book is set in Sabon LT Std

To Kathleen and Percy;
love always. The Bairn

Cast of Characters
(as written by Ida Finn)

———

Ida Finn – A maid with a secret. Nothing else to say. Who's asking, anyway? No more questions.

The Rat Prince – Ida's alter-ego, the infamous sneak thief, scourge of Loxport, devilishly good-looking.

Lucinda Belmonte – Ida's employer. Silly, shrill, harmless.

Lord Casterbury – Lucinda's paramour. Ida's nemesis.

Edith Webb – A maid at the Acutus Club. Bubbly, sweet, determined to befriend Ida (despite Ida's best efforts).

Clem Magnesan – A jeweller and inventor. Handsome in an overly cocky, chatty kind of way. Apparently.

Chapter One

———

Lucinda Belmonte still had the rosy complexion of a teenager. Ida supposed that was due to sleeping until noon most mornings.

'You look lovely tonight, ma'am,' Ida said, fussing with her mistress' hair. Lucinda turned away from the mirror to simper over her shoulder at her. If scientists put both Ida and Lucinda side by side in a museum, stuffed and posed, they would be a study in opposites; nineteen and thirty-five, one all ruffles and blonde curls, one serious and narrow with cropped-short, dark hair.

'You're such a sweetheart, Ida. Pass me my rouge, please – no, not that one! Honestly. Dusky rouge, with this dress?'

Ida murmured her apologies as she placed the little tub on her mistress' dresser.

'Thank you, darling. Now – for my centrepiece. Do you think this one…'

Lucinda brandished a Clementine Lepsum hairpin in Ida's direction, and the huge gem glinted between her fingers like a chunk of expensive toffee.

'…or this sweet little thing that Lord Casterbury gave me?'

In her other hand sat a golden butterfly brooch. One twist of its dial and the wings, set with rubies the size of Ida's thumbnail, would flutter prettily against her collarbone.

'He is accompanying me to the gala tonight, after all.'

Ida considered her options carefully.

'What about this?' She said, picking up a bronze pendant, set with peridot. 'I haven't seen you wear this one in a while, ma'am.'

Lucinda pushed her lips into a pout. 'That old thing?'

'Vintage pieces are all the rage, so I hear.'

Lucinda looked back to Lord Casterbury's brooch; brows furrowed in thought.

'Devon will be expecting…'

Ida knew what Devon Casterbury was expecting. She'd known for months that Lord Devon Casterbury was making a play for her childless, widowed – and stupefyingly rich – employer. And she also knew that hadn't stopped Casterbury from swatting Ida on the backside every time she served him tea. She looped the pendant around her mistress' neck.

'Isn't that a good reason not to wear it? If you see my meaning, ma'am.'

After a moment, Lucinda's lips curled into a sly smile.

'I see… Lord Casterbury needs to be more generous with his gifts, perhaps,' she tossed the brooch back onto her dresser. 'You're right, Ida. You always give such good advice!'

'I try, ma'am.'

The two women fell quiet – Lucinda putting the finishing touches to her ensemble, Ida folding the myriad of dresses strewn about the floor.

'You will lock the door tonight, Ida, dear?' Lucinda asked, viciously pinching colour into her cheeks.

'Yes, ma'am.' She always did.

'And make sure the windows are all closed before you go to bed; I don't want to come home to find myself face to face with that awful Rat Prince.'

Lucinda shuddered. The Rat Prince had been plaguing the city for three years, now – sneaking into well-to-do houses, helping himself to whatever he found before vanishing without a trace. No broken windows, no shattered locks, no calling card. The constables were beside themselves.

A brisk rapping at the door. Ida placed Lucinda's shoes in front of her feet and slipped downstairs to answer it. A broad, blond man in his mid-thirties stood in the doorway, his cheeks flushed, monocle glinting.

'Ahh, the scrumptious Ida.'

Ida tilted her head up, very slightly, to look him in the eye. She only came up to Devon Casterbury's lapels, but she would make good use of every molecule of her five foot two inches.

'Good evening, Lord Casterbury.'

'Hard at work, I hope?'

'Yes, Lord Casterbury.'

Casterbury looked Ida up and down. 'Good, good. I like a hard worker. Perhaps I'll steal you away from Ms. Belmonte for myself, what?'

Tall or short, skinny or curved – no matter what the body shape, Lord Devon Casterbury could always be trusted to find something to ogle. Ida dropped her gaze but held her ground. Lucinda descended the staircase, beaming.

'Lord Casterbury, darling.'

'My dearest Lucinda. You look utterly ravishing. An angel in rose silk.'

'Oh, Devon, you're such a poet!'

Ida suppressed the urge to roll her eyes. Casterbury kissed Lucinda's hand with a flourish – clasping her petite palm in his meaty fingers, his lips lingering against her skin. Then, his brow furrowed.

'You aren't wearing the rubies?'

Lucinda smiled her sickliest smile.

'Oh, but Devon. This little locket goes so well with my dress,' the pout made its return. 'I can go change, if you like?'

Casterbury straightened, flustered.

'Oh, no, of course not, my dear. My apologies – don't expect a mere mortal man like myself to know anything about fashion. Shall we?'

They swept away in Casterbury's brand new, gleaming horseless carriage – a Brightwind, as Casterbury was often fond of mentioning. Ida assumed that meant it was expensive. To her, it was just a tall, black brick of a contraption on iron wheels, puttering grey globs of smoke into the air as it moved. Once they were safely down the street, she took to her chores. She had to admit, looking after a widow was a lot easier than a family. Straighten a few linens, sweep the floors, blow out the candles as she went, and she was done.

With her work finished for the evening, she retired to her own quarters, high in the attic, where she changed out of her maid's dress into a pair of men's trousers and

4

a black tunic. A set of lockpicks slid into her pocket, and atop her head she fixed a pair of goggles, their bottle-green lenses snatching up the tiny amount of light in the room. They were the only thing she had left of her mam, and she wouldn't trade them for all the pictures and locks of hair in the world. One twist, and she could see in any condition, night or day.

That brooch had to go. Ida never stole from her employers as a rule, but this Casterbury character was worth the risk. Ida had more than a sneaking suspicion that her Lord-and-Master-to-be would be something of a snoop – and the notoriety of unmasking her and 'saving' his lady love would send a man like Casterbury into palpitations. Lucinda Belmonte was spoiled, silly and shrill, but she was harmless and naive. A nice facade for Ida's real career. Devon Casterbury was not going to spoil that. And if the object of his affections was careless enough to lose his gifts, well, perhaps he'd take them – and his horrible, ticklish moustache – elsewhere.

Lucinda would probably weep and scream and turn the house upside down looking for the butterfly, but Ida would wager she wouldn't even consider searching her maid's quarters, let alone accuse her. Oh no; sweet, darling Ida would never steal. She was a good girl.

Her middleman was meeting her at midnight, in the back alley behind The Lord and Horse Inn. But the night was still young, and Ida was determined to have some fun.

Out the window. Closing it carefully behind her, up the drainpipe and over the roof. She took off at a run, leaping soundlessly from rooftop to rooftop, cheekily landing on the canopy of a parked carriage before disappearing into the night, down one of the thousand cobbled streets that wound through the city of Loxport.

God, it felt good to be The Rat Prince again.

Chapter Two

———

Below her, the city. Her city. The warm orange flicker of the gaslit streetlamps in the Industrial Estates and the residential areas – blurred by the mist that rolled in from the River Lox; clashed against the eerie bioluminescent blue glow of the newly installed lamps in the more elite Scientific Estates; found especially, Ida noted, around the museums, the galleries, and the lecture halls. Very fancy.

Loxport was England's shining star when it came to 'The Scientific Arts' – the study of automata, of crypto-biology, and other strange half-magical sounding studies. Nestled away up in the North, far from the riff-raff, where knowledge and culture could flourish, money was funnelled into buildings where intelligent, well-bred people could get drunk, flirt, and gawk at each other's shiniest new toys. Ida couldn't have dreamed up a better city to prowl.

She settled herself on the shingles of her chosen rooftop and pushed her goggles off her face to enjoy the view. The Scientific Estates were pretty, but it wasn't where she was heading tonight. Anyone worth their salt in that part of town would identify Casterbury's little token quicker than she could blink. No; she was heading to the back streets, where people didn't know or care who ran the largest department store in the city.

The Lord and Horse Inn was known for being a sort of meeting place for the criminal community of the city. Big Della would break your legs for starting a fight or laying a hand on one of the younger girls pulling pints behind the bar, but she wasn't too bothered about deals being brokered or wagers being set as long as you kept a smile on your face and a civil tongue in your head.

Ida didn't know where the brooch was heading once money changed hands. She didn't much care. She just wanted it gone. She repositioned her goggles, adjusted them for the darkening evening, and turned her back on the glowing blue lamps.

Later, as she finished up her security sweep of the building after dropping off the brooch in her designated safe spot, she spied her middleman. He looked about fifteen. Gangly, awkward, and unsure. It certainly didn't help matters that he was swaddled up in a sailor's coat that looked a size too large for him. Lord almighty, Ida thought, Terry Powell's sent his bairn to do the pick-up. Terry was a true businessman – trading and selling any goods he got his hands on – but he was also nothing if not a family man. Look on the bright side; this should be fairly easy, at least. And, for once, there were no constables wandering up and down the streets, looking for something to do – or a fight to pick.

'Y'alright, Reg?'

Reggie Powell choked on the last of his cigarette as

The Rat Prince dangled his leg idly over the guttering of the stables next door to the Lord and Horse. The place ran a tidy trade getting various drunkards and nervous poets home after Last Call. Not everyone could afford a Horseless, especially in this part of the city. The horses snickered gently to themselves, as if in on the joke. The Rat Prince's eyes gleamed large and green as he sat, cool as you please, above Reggie's head. The lad nodded, trying to be nonchalant.

'Y-you got the brooch, mate?' he stuttered.

'Nah, I just thought I'd come out for a walk under the gas-light. And keep your voice down, eh? Some of us have an appointment with the constables we're trying to avoid.'

The Rat Prince crouched at the edge of the rooftop, knees wide, hands pressed against the shingles.

'Now,' he said, his voice raspy and soft, 'put your dad's money on the floor, and pick up your little present from behind those bins, there's a good lad.'

Reggie's breath left him in a heavy sigh of relief. His first job, clearly. 'Cheers, sir. It's a gift from my dad, to –'

'I don't really care, Reg. Just go get your trinket before I grow old here.'

Reggie placed the wedge of notes on the floor carefully, as though he thought it would explode. Ninety Athena-notes, as they agreed – a relative bargain for real rubies. Then, Reg turned to the bins that were tucked just around the corner of the inn behind him. As he bent to pick up the small object wrapped in brown paper, he heard a soft thump, like his Nana's cat jumping from a shelf. When he turned, The Rat Prince was already back on the roof, money in hand.

'So,' The Rat Prince said, checking the bills as he spoke, 'you striking out on your own, Reg? Want a little piece of the Night Market for yourself, like your dad?'

Reggie shrugged.

'Maybe. Dad wanted to see if I could manage a pick-up on my own, before I join the business. See if he can trust me, yeah?'

'Aye,' The Rat Prince said. 'Tell him I send my regards, Reg – or maybe he can hear me, since he's loitering inside by the back window, there. He thought he was being inconspicuous.'

The Rat Prince straightened.

'He's not.'

As Reggie whirled to find his father pretending to nurse a pint, The Rat Prince melted into the foggy shadows of a Loxport evening. No one was watching to see which way he went, which rooftops he leapt over to get home.

No one ever was.

Chapter Three

———

Ida had a secret addiction: one that helped her jump out of bed at dawn, with at least a semblance of enthusiasm, to start preparing the house for Lucinda's awakening.

Sugared almonds. When she started making a regular wage, they were the only treat that Ida allowed herself. Every Thursday, she went to the stalls on Potter's Way and bought herself two gold Athena's worth of sweets to get her through the coming week, along with whatever sugary delights Lucinda was craving. (Ten silver Hermes to one Athena; some banker a hundred years ago had this grand idea that the country's worship of knowledge needed to extend to the currency.) Anything more than that was too much money to spend on sweets; plus, Ida knew if she bought more, she'd just eat the lot in one go; thinking she could excuse it because she had more to spare.

Ida's Alarum timepiece began to chime at five in the morning: a veritable lie in, compared to some places that she'd worked. Because Lucinda lived alone, all Ida had to do was draw the curtains back, sweep the floors, light the fires, do some light dusting, collect the delivery of eggs and milk from the back door, set the internal copper pipes that warmed the house, and have a cup of tea waiting for Lucinda when she rose at midday. Easy.

The Alarum was placed over by Ida's washbasin, so she had to get up to pull down the little lever that stopped the accursedly cheerful chiming. Then, she'd stretch: if she'd had a particularly interesting night as The Rat Prince, this could make the difference between getting her jobs done quickly and standing on aching limbs as Lucinda lectured her on the importance of matching cup to saucer when serving tea.

'This cup is eggshell, Ida! The saucer is cream! Honestly!'

So Ida would massage her feet, roll through her spine, and stand on one foot until the gears of her Alarum had all aligned again, and the little white face said half past. Then, she'd slip on her black cap and work dress, and quietly begin her day.

She heard Lucinda before she saw her. A lot of women in Loxport expected a bath to be drawn before they awoke, so they could drift from slumber to apparently effortless beauty discreetly. Lucinda, luxuriating in her widowed, childless life, liked to wander downstairs, floor length robe flowing behind her, sip at her tea and nibble delicately on some brioche with jam, before gasping, hand to heart, and saying: 'Look at me, Ida! I'm not even dressed! Draw me a bath, there's a good girl...'

Ida had often thought about palming a few of the various tiny bottles that lined Lucinda's bathroom shelves. Bubble baths, beauty oils, scents from some of the finest perfumeries in the city, all unopened and forgotten about.

Lucinda liked to shop more than she liked to own, and they'd make Ida a nice little side earning: someone had always forgotten their wife's birthday, or their daughter was getting married unexpectedly and wanted to feel like Princess Victoria the Second for the day. But Ida had rules. 'Never shit where you sleep, hinny,' Mam always said. Last night was the exception that proved the rule. Ida was   prepared for the inevitable fallout of the loss of the brooch. But if she cringed around the house like a dog waiting to be whipped, she would put herself under suspicion. So, for the morning, she let herself forget about the whole thing.

Most of Lucinda's home was dressed up in the faintest petal-pink and dark burnished wood. Her drawing room always reminded Ida of the inside of a chocolate-strawberry fondant. But the kitchen was cool and crisp; blue and white tiles bringing out the gleaming copper of the heating pipes, which snaked across the room bare and shining. It wasn't worth the money to hide them just for the servants.

As she was setting up the teapot and taking the butter out of the chuntering, bitterly cold Algid Ice-Chest to soften, there was a knock at the door to the kitchen. Ida suppressed a sigh. It better not be Daniel. Please, please don't let it be Daniel. Lucinda's nephew fancied himself a bohemian and thought it incredibly jolly to loiter in the servant's areas of the house,   getting in the way. He was witty like that. Ida set the butter on its covered dish and opened the door.

It wasn't Daniel.

'Morning, Ida!' Edith chirped. She dipped into a playful curtsy, and the mass of red hair around her head bounced in greeting. She was all softness and bounce, was Edith Webb; large green eyes, round cheeks, swaying hips. And somehow, her maid's cap always stayed in place.

Edith worked at Casterbury's gents club, the Acutus – an elite group of scientists, artists, and great thinkers that owned a building on Minerva Avenue. It had a reputation for being the ultimate place for a young upcoming lord or brilliant student to mingle with their peers, bounce around theories and ideas, and create a culture of genius in the city. As far as Ida was concerned, it was a place for rich people to smoke, drink, eat, and argue. When Lucinda paid a visit, Ida stood in the corridor and kept herself amused by idly fiddling with the mechanical hat spinner in the hallway, playing probability games concerning which hat would flip out of its little cubby hole with which spin, until one of the maids had decided to become her friend. By force, if necessary.

It had started with quiet, conspiratorial offerings of a cup of tea. 'You're a guest here too, y'know?'

Ida had declined. But every time she waited for her mistress to get bored of being flirted at by a gaggle of Casterbury's cronies this same maid, the one with the big red curls, always seemed to be walking past on some errand or another. And she always – always! – made conversation.

'You again? Fancy a job while you wait?'

'It's Ida, isn't it? I'm Edith – suppose you should actually know my name since you see me so much.'

'She got you waiting out here again, Ida? Whatever they're talking about can't be that interesting…'

'Oh my god, Ida! They're still talking about that opera. Three weeks I've had to hear about that bloody play! I swear, if they try and sing that aria again I. Will. Scream.'

Ida didn't want friends. Friends were just another link in the chain that connected her to the constables. Someone to be questioned, to accidentally give up your name in an investigation – especially a girl who worked so closely with the very people Ida tended to rob. Friends were just another way to get caught. It was better to blend into the background, to be unassuming, invisible. But you couldn't be invisible if you made a maid cry by telling her to piss off, either. So, Ida became proficient in small nods and tight smiles, in letting Edith ramble on and giving up very little in return. And yet, somehow, that had led to the damned girl standing on her doorstep, a small brown parcel in her hand.

'Y'alright?' Edith asked. Ida shrugged, realising she hadn't actually spoken yet.

'Can't complain.'

'Oh, I can,' Edith laughed. 'They've got me on dinner shifts all week again. Your whole day is taken up: you spend the early morning just waiting to go to work, then the evening just making your own dinner then going to bed! Kate's just going to have to fend for herself, I suppose.'

Kate? Was that the grandmother? The dog? No, hang on: the sister. Little sister. Mother and father were dead. God, don't make that mistake out loud, Ida... wait, what was she saying now?

'...in the park. What do you think?'

'Um.'

Edith pouted.

'Oh, come on, Ida! It'll be fun. Get you away from this house for an hour or two. When's your day off, again? Wednesdays?'

She knew exactly when it was. Edith could retain information about a person's life like Ida could about the security of a building.

'... I suppose so, yes.'

'Mine too! What a coincidence! I'll come pick you up. Oh, and this,' Edith pressed the brown parcel into her hand, 'is for you.'

'Ida? Ida, what has happened to my tea?'

Lucinda. Edith waved manically from the bottom of the yard.

'Alright, I'll let you go, I'm off to work, byeeee!'

And she was gone. In the seconds before Lucinda descended upon the kitchen, Ida opened the package.

It was a bar of chocolate. Not as expensive as the stuff in Lucinda's pantry, but Ida knew the label. Sweets from Mimi's Chocolaterie were worth an Athena or two. There was only one shop, and it often sold out by day's end. Edith had got her this specially. Why?

'Good morning, Ida!'

Ida spun as her mistress entered the room.

'Good morning, ma'am. Did you sleep well?'

'Oh, I did, Ida – and after such a wonderful evening. Devon was such captivating company, and we danced all night and… what's that in your hand, Ida dear?'

Ida looked down at the bar in her hand.

'It… was on the doorstep this morning, ma'am. Perhaps Mimi's are trying a new way to drum up sales? A free sample?'

'Oooh – or perhaps it's from a secret admirer! How mysterious,' Lucinda sighed, as Ida set the chocolate down next to her mistress' plate and poured her a cup of tea.

Chapter Four

———

'…And it was so wonderful to see dear Eloise looking so well again; I've told you she was dealing with a fever?'

'Yes, ma'am.'

'I'll have to make my way over there for tea one day soon. My poor brother. Dealing with the paper, while his only daughter was ill, without a wife to support him. She's so clever, you know, my Eloise, with her little animal sculptures. And that Daniel, I wager he was no help, no help at all! I swear, Ida – Christopher has given that boy everything, everything he could want – and what does he have to show for it? An heir with no interest in the Loxport Express that gallivants all over the city, writing poems, Ida! Poems!'

'Should I turn him away when he next calls, ma'am?'

'Oh, no, Ida, I never said that – he is terribly fun company, after all. And so handsome!'

Lucinda leaned over her teacup, a pantomime of girlish slyness.

'Don't you think my nephew is handsome, Ida?'

No, Ida thought. I think he's a foppish, loud, arrogant peacock that needs a good slap.

'Yes,' Ida said, 'I suppose so, ma'am. He has your

family's good looks.'

'He looks like his mother, not Christopher and I,' Lucinda laughed. 'Both he and his sister – that   gorgeous brown skin, which will at least save Daniel from losing his pallor to worry by the time he's twenty-five, like Christopher did. Jonathan always used to say…'

Lucinda stopped, her hands frozen mid-gesture. After a long moment, she gently raised her teacup to her lips, and took a long sip, her eyes closed.

Ida knew better than to ask her to continue. She'd barely known Jonathan Belmonte – she'd been hired for the position two months before he passed away. She had no fond memories of the man. He was a decent, polite employer, to be sure, but he saw her the same way all her employers had: a piece of useful furniture, like a grandfather clock or an automated shoe shiner. After the funeral, Lucinda shut herself in her room for a fortnight, only opening the door to accept Ida's offerings of food and tea and to listen blankly as she was informed of sympathy cards that had been posted through the door. Then, one morning, Lucinda opened her door and called for Ida to draw her a bath. And that was that. Time, and their lives, went on: Lucinda's silly, vain, frivolous personality returned. But they never spoke of the dearly departed man of the house. And then, weeks after Lucinda's black dresses went back into the wardrobe after her year-long mourning period, Devon Casterbury began circling the house like a Kraken scenting blood.

'Anyway!' Lucinda continued, plonking her cup down on

the saucer, 'I have a splendid idea for a day out, Ida dear!'

Oh, no.

'Ma'am,' Ida began, 'I have so much to do today. The egg-man is coming back for his five Athenas, I was just about to start airing the second floor…'

'There's an outdoor exhibition happening at the Schuyler Museum! There'll be automata, and art, and jewellery…'

Ida's ears pricked up, despite herself.

'It's the opening day today, and everyone knows the most fascinating events are near the beginning, and I simply can't go alone…'

Ida had worked in houses with ladies' maids before. Pretty, prissy girls that thought themselves better than Ida because their dresses were flouncier. But, in the Belmonte household, Ida was a maid for all occasions. So, after more badgering, Ida abandoned her chores to run a bath for Lucinda and, in the interim, find 'a nice dress for stepping out in' somewhere in the empty chasm of her wardrobe. All she had was a purple thing with black buttons down the front. It would do.

The more affluent parts of Loxport – where the rich and educated worked, lived and played – were dominated by wide streets lined with trees that sprinkled their blossoms on the pavement, and houses that had a substantial amount of space between them, stretching out long back gardens behind them. Children played with kites shaped like dirigibles, youths sped about on gleaming velocipedes thinking they were rebellious, and constables sauntered about with nothing much to do but look incredibly suave and important. Nothing like where Ida had grown up. As they neared the Scientific Estates, the buildings rose high and tall in the spring sunshine, gleaming and clean, full of students, entrepreneurs and learned people. This city was always growing, always adding new buildings to streets and new halls to those buildings and putting new and shiny toys inside those halls. It would never be finished, never quite be beautiful or sophisticated enough.

The Schuyler Museum was one of the most prestigious places of public learning in Loxport, outside of the universities. It looked, from the outside, exactly like Ida imagined a palace to look; imposing and grand on its man-made hill, made of shining white stone, with a courtyard and a pearly fountain stretching out before it. The steps up to the museum itself were marble, as were the columns, carved with the shape of Krakens, the museum's mascot, wrapping around them. Ida had been inside exactly once, a job that had involved stealing a live exhibit while the elites of Loxport held a fundraiser in the very next room. She'd been paid handsomely, though the experience of hauling what amounted to a large and inexplicably valuable frog in an earthenware jar up a ladder is one she would   prefer never to repeat. But the Schuyler in the light of day – and, in particular, this day – was a markedly different experience.

The museum itself shimmered in the midday sun, as hordes of Loxport citizens milled around the huge courtyard. More constables stood at each corner, watching in case a negotiation over pricing turned nasty, but mostly to look at the pretty, posh girls in their pretty, posh skirts. They had a pretty easy life, the constables, their policing tactic seemed to mostly involve dishing out concerned and thoughtful looks to wealthy victims, stern glares and baton-waggling at the odd petty thief they did catch, and scratching their heads over the more prolific ones who, more often than not, were laughing at them in a pub around the corner as they counted their share of the spoils. People like Terry Powell, who had a whole network of lackeys and middlemen to keep him out of trouble; though he'd do well to install some of his more discreet habits into his son after his encounter with The Rat Prince the other night. Bloody Reg.

She could see the tops of the exhibit tents as they approached – with the crowd obscuring their bases, they looked almost like dirigibles, about to take off. Lucinda squealed with delight, grabbing Ida's hand as they moved forward, into the throng of people.

Everywhere Ida looked, there was something new to see, someone else shouting or laughing.

'Come see the wonders of the far-off, mysterious South! That, miss, is a Black Shuck pup – oh, careful where you put your fingers, sir, they do bite…'

'Absolutely fascinating, old sport – yes, yes, I shall have to read your paper on the matter…'

'Madam, I assure you: in two years, every home will have one. All the freedom of your own two feet, with the speed and efficiency of your horseless carriage…'

'I'm sure your brother would love to invest! Here – let me just give you my office address…'

In the midst of this commotion, Ida was distracted by a stall full of glimmering gems and jewellery. She managed to slip her hand free of Lucinda's. Her mistress disappeared into the crowd, and Ida took the opportunity to look over the glittering scraps of stone on display. Some she knew – rubies, Lepsum, strings of pearls – some even she had never seen before. A lanky, clean-shaven boy of about her age, wearing a purple waistcoat and messy strawberry-blond hair that was longer than the fashion, leaned on the opposite side of the stall, his smile as bright as his wares.

'Beautiful jewels for sale, today! Rubies, Orthoclase, Purple Lepsum – sourced from all over the world, just got a new vein of Peridot in for this very occasion! Perfect for both the love of your life and the invention of your dreams, sets beautifully into clockwork, smooth as silk! Anything you like there, sir? For an additional fee I can set it for you – I must admit I am an extremely talented gent…'

Ida took a step forward. The 'talented gent' winked at her, making a clicking noise with his tongue. Ida pulled back, horrified, but something green and shiny at the end of the table caught her eye. A thin rod, about the length from her middle finger to her wrist. The colour was amazing – it started off as the bright, almost shocking green of grass in spring, then faded to a gentle, almost cool mint. The gent behind the   table waggled his fingers in Ida's face.

'Y'alright, there, miss?'

She jumped; he was a little closer than she'd thought. He beamed. Ida disliked him.

'Gorgeous, isn't it? Never had anything like that before in my orders – must've been put in by accident. A unique beauty is a real rarity in these bustling times, I find! I'm hoping one of these educated and esteemed fellows can tell me exactly what it is, so I can adjust my price accordingly.' Ida nodded.

'Very pretty.'

'And I know pretty when I see it,' the man said, winking again with an insufferable smirk. 'But – oh, now hang on…'

The gent scanned his table, before snatching up a scrap of Purple Lepsum on a simple copper chain. 'Yep – this would go beautifully with your dress. And your eyes, if I do say so.'

Ida's eyes were brown. Not chocolate-brown, or mahogany-brown. Dried-mud-brown. Unvarnished-wood-brown. They didn't go with anything. Besides, Ida could tell the chain was cheap. Or, at least,   cheaper than the gem. He'd pegged her for a servant. Correctly, of course. But still, it irked her.

'My name's Clem,' the gent said. 'Clem Magnesan, gemologist – a term I patented myself, don't believe the naysayers. And you are…?'

'Why should I tell you?'

'Well, aren't you a peach?' Clem Magnesan grinned. 'I

always like to know the names of my sparring partners.'

'It's a secret.'

'I love secrets.'

'Well, let me know when you crack the enigma.'

'It'll take me years, I'm sure. Decades, even.'

'Oh, Ida, darling, there you are!' Lucinda appeared as if from the ether and grabbed her wrist. 'You simply have to see this adorable dancing girl! Well, she isn't a girl, she's an automaton. Mister McConnell has outdone himself again…'

As she was dragged away into the crowd, Ida looked back at the thin gem on the table. The gent bowed, his smile just bordering on mockery.

Chapter Five

―――――

Ida watched the dancing automaton. She picked at the stick of spun sugar Lucinda handed her when she got bored with it, fragments sticking to the roof of her mouth. She talked Lucinda out of buying a shoal of baby Hippocamps from a stall lined with glass cubes full of fish and Cryptids ('They grow rather large, ma'am. I think these are more for professional collectors with *space*'). She was spun around a hundred different ways, asked and begged and demanded to look at *this*, and *this*, and *this*...

And then it got worse.

'Devon said he would be here by two,' Lucinda said, tucking her skirts in around her, as she sat on the edge of one of the marble seats carved into the fountain's edge. Ida wondered if it contained enough water to drown herself in. She had not been informed that Casterbury was to be part of the day's festivities. Not that she could have refused to come, but that wasn't the point. She could have prepared herself for -

'Ah, there is my radiant spring flower!'

Oh god. Lucinda was blushing. Ida wanted to vomit.

Devon Casterbury didn't need a cane. But today, he

walked with one, tucking under his arm like a baton.

The gem at the hilt shimmered; Tyrenite-blue, Ida noted. He was dressed in clothes that, on a better man, would have been flattering, even chic. Grey trousers with a fine checked pattern, and a frock coat in a similar colour over a rich blue waistcoat, silver pocket watch chain glinting in the sun. The splash of colour was very on trend with Loxport men, Ida knew; The Rat Prince had robbed a tailor about a month ago. However, on Casterbury's broad frame, they looked performative; like the clothes of a man desperate to keep up with fashion, no matter what the fashion was. Lucinda, though she was about the same age as Casterbury, looked far more at home in her skin. Even her copper rose hairpin, something usually seen on girls ten years her junior, looked endearing and subtle. *Unlike the woman wearing it*, Ida smirked, after catching herself complimenting her employer with a hint of embarrassment.

Lucinda leapt to her feet, and Casterbury spun her around, her skirts billowing and threatening to take out passers-by. You'd think they hadn't seen each other in months. She planted a kiss on his cheek, and then Casterbury turned to Ida.

'And the effervescent Ida! How are you today, my girl?' He swept her hand up in his, lips parted. *You're not here*, Ida thought, panic draping over her shoulders like a cold, wet blanket, *this isn't happening, you're on a rooftop just as the sun sets and the breeze is up and don't pull your hand away don't pull your hand away.*

DON'T –

Casterbury's lips connected with Ida's *palm*, not the back of her hand, her palm, as he bowed to her, swinging his other arm out behind him. His moustache was damp. Ida felt her cheeks growing crimson with fury. *Excellent: make a big performance of how well you treat the help, Devon dear, by humiliating them in front of strangers.* And, worst of all, because she couldn't kick him square in the jaw, Devon would think the blush was because she was flattered. Ugh.

'Good morning, Lord Casterbury,' she managed.

Luckily, Casterbury's attention had already wandered.

She could seethe quietly to herself as she walked behind the pair as they went around the exact same stalls she had already seen today.

'Lucinda, my dear, my old chum Valentine's boy is here somewhere, selling these ingenious new fountain pens equipped with a conductive coil inside, you see, so the ink, when warmed, dries all the quicker on the page. Very expensive, very chic, what?'

'Oh, what a clever young man!'

Ida stared at the back of her mistress' dress and tried not to imagine her bustle bursting into flames. Not fifteen minutes prior, Lucinda had been dragging Ida around this courtyard, gripping her wrist so tightly that she still had pale marks on her skin where the blood wasn't circulating yet. And now, because 'Dear Devon' was around, Ida was little more than an accessory.

Again. She was just as smart as any of these puffed-up buffoons in their expensive clothes, and she made her money without putting on some stupid show for other, equally puffed-up buffoons. She had no inherited wealth to buffer a bad choice or a wrong move. Just her own two feet, and her brain.

'...the opera next Saturday night. Miranda Clarke is an absolute sensation in the role, and I thought we could have dinner at La Niche afterwards? I have been meaning to sample their truffle gnocchi for some time now.'

'That sounds wonderful, Devon. Ida, remember that for me, dear.'

'Yes, ma'am.'

Ida wondered if she could arrange any jobs for that night. Maybe Terry Powell's lad wanted a little more education. That could be a laugh.

'And,' Casterbury said, tickling Lucinda under the chin, 'why don't you co-ordinate your little outfit to match my brooch, this time? I'm sure you will look utterly ravishing.'

Lucinda giggled.

'Perhaps, Devon, perhaps...'

Ida stopped herself from laughing by taking great interest in the stalls around her. Their romance had a week left, at most. Then she could go back to her much simpler, quieter, less harassed life.

As this thought crossed her mind, Ida made eye contact with the lanky, messy-haired lad across the crowded courtyard. He clocked her, and who she was with. He grinned. Ida shook her head.

Don't. You. Dare, she mouthed. Somehow, his grin grew even wider.

'Hallo-oo there, Ida!' he called, waving frantically. 'My dear old friend, haven't seen you in an age! Enjoying the exhibition?'

Lucinda whirled.

'Ida, do you know someone here?'

'No.'

'Ida! Hallo-ooo there! It's me, Clem!'

'Devon, let's go see what Ida's friend is showcasing!'

Oh, for god's sake.

Clem vaulted over his stall to clasp Lucinda's hand in his own. He was surprisingly agile, for someone so leggy. 'Ida, who is this stunning young lady? Your employer's daughter, perhaps?'

'*Oh, my*!'

And so, Ida found herself standing sullenly beside Lucinda as Clem Magnesan, gemologist, showed off his very shiniest trinkets. He was now leaning over his table again, holding a square, multicoloured stone on a silver chain up to an enraptured Lucinda. He reminded Ida of Daniel, Lucinda's nephew; silver-tongued and pleased with himself.

'Now, this, Madam, is Bismuth; see how the light catches on the myriad of surfaces? A lot of your... *less inspired* jewellers will set the gem within a larger piece, using metal or wire to add to the complexity. I feel – and this may just be the musings of a humble gemologist, so you must excuse me, Madam – that one must marry the gem to a clean, simple design, in order to let true, natural beauty show through.'

Clem looked up through his eyelashes, tongue poking out between his lips as he smirked, and Lucinda tittered. She was in the palm of his hand, and her purse was in hers. Ida had to admit this Clem character was good. And his wares were pretty nice, too. She could imagine getting twice his asking price at the Night Market, especially for something as strange to look at as this 'Bismuth'. She'd have to file that word away for later use. It wasn't often someone could teach Ida a thing or two about shiny, valuable objects.

'I say, my boy,' Devon Casterbury bellowed, 'what do you make of this, then?'

He tapped his cane sharply upon Clem's table top, rattling a set of opal earrings as he did. Lucinda blinked, as if she'd forgotten Casterbury was with them. Clem gracefully raised the tip of the cane up with his long fingers and examined the sky-blue gemstone.

'Hm. Tyrenite, if I'm not mistaken, sir? A very nice gem, with a lot of... er, flash. I'd have made a little more of this vein of jet-black running through it – see how it's off to the side, near the setting? - but that's neither here nor there. But next time you are in want of a cane, do come my way, I have a smithy down on Sixpence Street...'

'Quite,' Casterbury interrupted, accompanied by a well-bred sniff of disdain. His attempt at showing off clearly hadn't gone the way he intended. 'Lucinda, my love, shouldn't we be going? Odessa Malko is giving a lecture at four, and I wouldn't want to miss it.'

'In a *moment*, Devon dear. I do think I'd like to buy that Bismuth necklace, Clem *darling*…'

'An *excellent* choice, Madam. Thank you so very much for your patronage.' He was even mimicking her style of talking, those silly little inflections Lucinda put on her words. She spoke as if she was on the stage, projecting her emotions to the galleries.

'And perhaps something else; I do so like to be seen supporting the *local arts*…'

'So what is that stone, then, my boy?' Casterbury said, pointing with his cane at the thin green gem Ida had noticed earlier. 'I can't say I know the cut, or the…erm, the facets.'

Clem's smile faltered slightly.

'Oh…yes. My apologies, sir, I will have to find you later in the day to tell you. It was a fortuitous accident – it came as part of an order of Peridot last night, but Peridot it is definitely not. It could be something very rare, and so for now I have it on display purely in the hope it attracts someone well versed in…'

'I'll take it,' Casterbury said, flinging a sizeable wad of ten-Athena notes down on the table. Ida's mouth watered.

'Sir, it's not valued yet. I'll most likely have it on sale later in the exhibition–'

'Name a price.'

For the first time, Clem's smile had a forced, brittle angle to it. He pulled the green rod back towards him and under the table.

'Sir, I'm sorry, but I would like to learn what it is for myself, first. I do apologise, again, but I could put your name down as a potential buyer, once I…'

'A shame,' Casterbury said, stuffing his notes back into the pocket of his coat, 'you could have had Devon Casterbury, of Casterbury Emporiums, as a client. It could have led to grand things for your little business. I was sure you'd welcome the endorsement. Come along, Lucinda.'

And off he strode, leaving Lucinda to try and catch up while clutching the chain in her hand. Ida looked back at Clem before she followed and he shrugged, hands splayed.

'Moneyed folks, am I right?' he said. In that second, there was nothing of the showman in him; just a tired young man, trying to earn a living. Ida shook her head in a way she hoped was empathetic and loped off after her mistress.

Chapter Six

———

Devon Casterbury was not interested in the Matriarchal Social Studies of the Kraken (Marinus maximus). However, he sat stoically through the entire lecture, as a handsome woman with white-blonde hair in a silver waistcoat and dark grey trousers spoke on her research into the museum's mascot. Ida recognised Odessa Malko from the Acutus Club – profoundly serious, very grand, able to make a room fall silent with one raised eyebrow. She'd discovered the type of plankton that was used to power the Bioluminescent lights around the Scientific Estates. She was a genius. Ida knew all of this because Edith talked about her during her corridor monologues. Frequently.

As soon as Professor Malko had ceased talking and the applause had faded to a polite murmur, Casterbury stood, took Lucinda's arm and escorted her out, with Ida scrambling to make sure her mistress hadn't left anything behind.

'Devon, darling,' Lucinda said, 'I'd like to talk to Odessa. She just got back, and I haven't seen her for months!'

Lucinda tried to pull her hand free, but Casterbury's grip remained firm. Ida noticed with a spike of irritation that the pressure from his fingers was turning Lucinda's skin from rose-petal pink to red, before checking herself and focusing on the small cloth bags Clem had placed her purchases in.

'You'll see her at the club, my dear,' Casterbury replied. 'You won't have time to talk properly, with all the rabble here. I'll write to her, ask her to pop along.'

'Well… I suppose you're right. It is loud in here, after all.'

Ida looked around. Apart from a gaggle of girls about her own age at the back, giggling into their hands and shooting shy glances at the scientist, no one here looked particularly rabble-like. But Lucinda let herself be escorted home.

As the couple kissed goodbye and renewed their promises to meet on Saturday for the opera, Ida hopped nimbly into the safety of the hallway, away from the trajectory of any other farewell gestures. As the door closed on the seventeenth declaration of how much she'd be missed, Lucinda swept off her coat and handed it to Ida. There was a pause. Lucinda's face fell. For a moment, the cheerfulness went out of her like air from a punctured dirigible.

'He… he was just tired,' she said, avoiding her maid's gaze. 'It's hard for him to be away from the Emporium for long periods. He's a businessman, not a socialite. I have to respect that.'

Ida nodded as tactfully as she could. Lucinda could justify anything she wanted for as long as she liked. Between whatever the hell had happened between Clem and Casterbury at the exhibition, and the incoming storm of Lucinda having 'lost' the ruby butterfly brooch, Ida didn't think it mattered what conclusion her mistress came to. Plus, it wasn't exactly her place to respond with 'No, Lucinda. He isn't a socialite. He is an embarrassing, addle-pated blunderbuss, and I could have pilfered his pocket watch right off the chain six times today alone.'

Lucinda spun on her heel and stalked off up the stairs into the depths of the house.

'I require a cup of tea, Ida. And a biscuit. One of the toffee ones.'

The rest of the day proceeded much like any other. Ida entertained herself with chores on whatever floor of the house Lucinda was not occupying until around six, where she made herself a quick dinner from the remains of Lucinda's meal from the previous night – roast chicken – which Ida ate atop the last wedge of a soft, oily bread Lucinda loved from the Italian quarter of the Potter's Way market. Lucinda always asked Ida to buy far too much food for a household of one, and so there was an unspoken agreement that anything she grew bored of would be 'cleared away' by her maid. Not that anything she ate seemed to touch her frame. Ida hadn't put on much weight since she was a child. It was probably unhealthy, but Ida chalked it up to her nightly exploits and thought no more about it. As if she had time to fuss over her shape like Lucinda, or become fashionably ample like Edith.

Ida prepared Lucinda's food; smoked haddock, with

a variety of garden vegetables, boiled and served with herbs. The copper pipes, bare on the walls and shining with condensation, sang briskly to themselves while Ida chopped and seasoned. Her mam had drilled the basics of how to use a stove and kiln into her when she was small – but her ability with basil and tarragon was based purely on her employer's tastes. She wasn't even sure she'd like garlic if it wasn't for Lucinda's fondness of it.

Their evening routine was as well-choreographed as a ballet: Ida would place the food on the table and make herself scarce just as the lady of the house swept into her dining room to enjoy her food alone. Of course, Ida was not asked to stay. Then, as Lucinda retired to read for an hour or two, Ida would collect the dishes, wash up, and hang around the house doing odd jobs until Lucinda's call of 'Goodnight, Ida dear,' rang through the house.

'Goodnight, ma'am.'

Ida extinguished the candles, and waited another half hour. Then the real fun began. She – or rather, The Rat Prince – emerged into a city of fog. Thick, grey tendrils were coming in off the sea, swallowing up the ports, wrapping their tendrils around the   Industrial Estates. Unseasonal, for spring. Ida quickly moved from her own rooftop – didn't want anyone drawing conclusions – and stopped atop a house a street or two away. She drew the night air deep into her lungs, hoping to catch some of that cool North Sea mist along with it. Finally. Casterbury and his ego, Lucinda and her frippery, Edith and her constant friendliness; none of that mattered now. All that   mattered for the rest of the night was her speed, her wits and the space between one building and the next as she flew over the city.

She had no pressing errands, tonight, and so she indulged in a little light pickpocketry. Tying her goggles to a chimney pot, safely out the way, she drifted through a pub, lifting watches, matchbooks, a pretty ornate penknife that was probably someone's memento mori of a dearly departed Grandad, oh well, shouldn't have taken it to The Proud Piglet on a night of drinking, should they?

Attention, Ida had found, was a limited resource – especially when your target was drunk, or leering at the barmaid, or two harsh words away from a scrap. She was a small girl; she had to slip past men a lot larger than she was to get to the bar. She'd place a hand on their arm, or their shoulder blade, telegraphing where she was, while her other hand slipped into their back pocket, or around their wrist. It was almost too easy.

She ducked behind an opium den at one point as two constables wandered past, stepping in sync with each other. That probably took some rehearsal. They didn't actually check in the den to make sure everyone was behaving themselves, of course.

When she got bored, she recovered her goggles and hopped through the affluent residential part of Loxport; the Crescents and the Avenues and the Ways, where comfortably well-off families felt safe to leave their windows open. Ida rarely took from these houses, it was more of a test, a way to keep her senses sharp. She'd hide in an apple tree at the bottom of the expansive garden, watch the family come and go, and plan how she'd lift Mama's pearls from the nightstand before she could miss them. Then, her pockets and her soul both feeling full, she'd take off for her last errands of the night.

The Night Market, unlike Potter's Way, was not a physical place with actual stalls and barkers plying their wares. It was more a web of connections. Your cousin might drink in a pub where a man behind the bar knew someone who could make sure your business partner met with a tragic accident, or make those contracts of his vanish, or seduce his wife into giving up secrets. For the most part, everyone existed in a fairly stable truce; it was like an ecosystem that supported foxes and crows and alley-cats alike… and rats, of course. And anyone who wished to purchase the services of this particular rat had to know how to contact him.

Ida had little cubbies stashed throughout Loxport, a disused storm drain here, a loose stone in a wall there. She checked them all; nothing tonight. How boring. Still, she thought, flipping the penknife in one hand as she stood in a back alleyway on Salt Street, near the ports, not a bad night for a scoundrel. The knife was nice. She supposed she'd keep it.

A sudden clattering from the entrance to the alley made her crouch behind a coal bunker. Someone was calling to his mate as he staggered into the dark street.

'Nah, mate, I'll just be a second – just gotta leave this

note for him, then we'll go to the Lord an' Horse.'

A slurred voice followed the first; 'Oh, aye. Hoping Peggy Coe is working tonight, Reggie? Like you've got a chance with a lass like her, anyways…'

'Aye, aye, whatever, mate. I'll charm her quick enough when I'm flush with Athenas. Some posh git paid me a canny amount to make sure The Rat Prince gets this –'

Reggie Powell's words were choked off as The Rat Prince himself leapt from the shadows and yanked him down behind the coal bunker. For a small, young-sounding bloke, Reggie thought as his head connected with the brick, The Rat Prince was damn strong. A blade pressed against his throat.

'Bugger me, Reg; keep your voice down,' a voice hissed.

'Oh hell! Sorry s-s—'

'Were you about to call me 'sir', Reg? You think I'm some sort of lord? Are you a total idiot?' The Rat Prince's huge, round, green eyes swam in front of Reggie's face, blocking out everything else in his vision.

'N-no, sir – I mean! Um…'

The Rat Prince threw him to one side, hopped up onto the coal bunker, and used it to jump onto the brick wall.

'Shut up. You drunk, Reg? Not very subtle for a Powell, is it? Want me to tell your dad about that next time we do a deal?'

The boy's face went pale, and then red.

'Well then, give me this message you were bellowing about and bugger off.'

Reggie held it up, swaying.

'Put. It. On. The. Bunker. Reg,' The Rat Prince growled. Reggie did so. Only once he and his mate had wandered off to the next drinking hole did the dark figure crawl down onto the bunker, snatch up the note, and vault away over half the city. Honestly, what was the Night Market coming to if Reggie Powell was the heir to the throne?

Chapter Seven

———

Nestled against a copper heating pipe on top of some tiny theatre just outside the moneyed part of Loxport, Ida pushed her goggles off her face, broke the seal – gold wax, very nice – and read the criteria for her next adventure in thievery. She suddenly realised she was in need of something fun, something a bit challenging. Lifting penknives and brooches was a little too easy.

Approximately thirty seconds later, she threw her head back in exasperation. Her skull met the pipe with a very satisfying bong noise. She raked her hands through what there was of her hair, yanking at the roots. Below her, she could hear the rapturous applause of the audience. Well, she had just asked for a challenge. Looking up at the shreds of mist passing overhead, she groaned at no one.

'You have to be joking.'

Chapter Eight

––––––

The Schuyler museum at night was a cross between a fairy garden and a circus. The tiniest lanterns had been wrapped around the Kraken pillars (if you followed the trail of their wiring to the back of the museum, you'd find a huge generator, noisily puffing out clouds of steam to power those delicate lights), and shards of glass and metal had been hung from the trees at the edges of the courtyard to reflect the light back onto the evening's guests, who milled from stall to stall in a similar manner to Ida, Lucinda and Casterbury hours before.

Casterbury. Bloody, bloody, pissing Casterbury.

Ida sat atop the Schuyler, behind the lip of concrete that kept the dirt, pigeon's nests and ventilation grates from the view of any of the surrounding lecture halls. She idly fiddled with the dials of her goggles; opening and closing the apertures, zooming in and out on the stall below her. Clem was chatting up a lady with a tiny, lace-covered top hat fascinator atop her perfectly coiffed head. The green rod was still at his side, without an identifying label. Evidently, he had yet to find an expert in his field to tell him what it was.

And Devon Casterbury wanted her to steal it. Wanted

to pay her – Ida swallowed – two thousand Athenas to steal it.

She could do it, obviously, and she'd make nearly as much as she made in a year from thievery. And astronomically more than she made making Lucinda's tea and washing her dishes. But she'd be doing him a favour in the process. Him.

He was obviously trying to impress Lucinda with some cockamamie attempt at masculinity via wealth, and that could put a significant dent in her plans to have him gone sooner rather than later. And, besides, she kept her Rat Prince life decidedly separate from her cover as a maid. She always had.

But still. Two. Thousand. Athenas.

Ida took the note, and its new companion written in her own hand, out of her pocket. Of course, it had taken Devon Casterbury half a page to get to the point of what he wanted with The Rat Prince. He'd waffled on endlessly about his Emporium, his prestige; given fawning, faux-flattering compliments about The Rat Prince's cunning, the stories of his infamous exploits. If she didn't hate the constables even more than she hated Devon Casterbury, Ida could take this letter to the nearest station and topple the entire Casterbury empire with one anonymous tipoff.

But she wanted those two thousand Athenas.

The night ended with someone wheeling that dancing automaton onto the steps of the Schuyler, while a man played a violin in accompaniment to the tune that flowed out from the music box she stood on.

I am your humble servant, love,

I am in your thrall.

So, let me dance you my devotion,

for I have no words at all…

As he drew his bow over the strings, the silver girl jittered to life and began to bend and twist her legs, raising her arms over her head. Some of the patrons stopped to watch, while others swept up their paramours and began to dance. Ida watched as their dresses billowed out like flowers on a pond, adding up the value of the jewellery she could see glittering in the light. Most of the vendors took this time to start shutting down their exhibits. Clem, however, didn't. He leaned on his table, fist against his jaw, and watched the dancing. He looked so quiet. So contemplative.

High above the crowd, Ida found herself watching him. Wondering what he was thinking. Probably trying to work out where those beautiful people get their earrings and their necklaces. Did he say his smithy was on Sixpence Street? That would be Lucinda's next 'day out'; the street with the taxidermist and the pottery shop that sculpted vases shaped like women's…

The violinist finished his aria with a flourish, and the crowd applauded. Clem snapped out of whatever daydream he was in and began putting his wares in a worn leather trunk behind his stall, grinning and calling to the guests as if they were old friends.

'Have a wonderful evening, ladies! Thank you again

for the commission, sir – ready by the weekend, I assure you, your cufflinks will be a sensation…'

Ida sat for the next three-quarters of an hour as he and the rest of the stall owners wheeled their wares in cases, trunks and on covered plinths inside of the Schuyler. She listened as they called to each other about how their day went, who may be interested in buying or investing, wishing each other luck. They must have designated a room for housing the exhibits for the duration. And, to Ida's delight, now that the crowds of important people had gone home, so had the constables. Easy enough, then: she'd slip into the museum the same way she did during the Infamous Frog Incident, pick the lock on the case, and be gone before the night's end. But not tonight. Something 'going missing' on the first night was far too suspicious. It was a risk, but Ida wasn't too concerned with another cat burglar getting to her prize first. Loxport's underbelly was full of common crooks and cut purses. But there was no one like The Rat Prince.

Ida slid down the drainpipe, up a neighbouring apple tree and onto a nearby rooftop to observe the guard's locking up routine. Seemed that they started at the roof, then worked their way down to the foyer, where they'd settle in for the night with a hot cuppa and a cigarette, no doubt. Easy enough.

She glanced at her own note one last time before setting off for the coal bunker on Salt Street. She hated Devon Casterbury. But money had no allegiances.

Dear Sir,

I will accept your commission. Anticipate another missive when the artefact is ready for collection. Payment will be expected that night.

Yours,
RP.

Chapter Nine

———

Wednesday. Ida's day off. Of course, it meant she had to work twice as hard the night before; making sure her absence wouldn't be noticed in the dust on the mantel, or the marks on the glass. Lucinda insisted she didn't need a replacement just for one day.

'It gives me a chance to hone my skills as a homemaker, Ida dear,' she said proudly, which meant laying an evening table of cold fish, bread and multiple cakes while congratulating herself on a job well done. Ah, well. Let her have her fun. And it wasn't like Ida wasn't around if things went horribly south with the dessert forks. Apart from the early morning, when Ida made a quick trip down to Tarnish Street and back, her idle days were spent in her room. She'd pull double duty on her stretches, get out her box of practice locks and polish up her picking skills for a while before breakfast. Perhaps flip through a penny dreadful she'd picked up at the market last time she was there, tossing sugared almonds into her mouth all the while. Peace, perfect peace.

A muffled bang from downstairs as the front door was thrown open.

'Hello? Aunt Lucinda? Ha-llo-ooh?'

Perfect. Absolutely perfect.

'Aunt Lucinda? You really shouldn't leave your front door open if you aren't in, you know…'

Ida hurriedly threw on her day uniform over her vest and headed downstairs. In the foyer, looking around him as if Lucinda might leap from behind a potted plant, was a tall, devastatingly handsome idiot of about twenty. His soft, brown skin looked just as fresh as ever, despite all his various vices that would drain a lesser man. His clothes, though expensive, were rumpled and creased, and his tight curls of ear-length hair clearly hadn't seen a steam-and-comb in a day or two. Ida gritted her teeth.

'Good morning, Master Daniel.'

'Ida, I've told you,' Lucinda's nephew said, waving her away as she tried to take his coat, 'I've told you, time and again, there is no need to stand on ceremony with me. Daniel will do…'

He turned to her, blinked, and looked down at her with round eyes.

'You haven't got any shoes on.'

Ida exhaled, long and slow.

'I'm technically not working today, Master Daniel. But I will happily tell Ms. Belmonte that you are here, if you would like to sit in the drawing room…'

'Capital idea, Ida; simply capital!' Daniel said, sauntering through the house and flinging himself onto a chaise lounge. His long legs kicked up into the air like an automaton threatening to malfunction. 'While we wait for her, would you be an angel and fry off a little bit of bacon for me? Just a little. With an egg. And some toast. Please.'

Typical Daniel Fawcett. Go out for a night – or three – of drinking and carousing in Loxport's rowdiest pubs and lushest opium dens, romancing anyone he could get his hands on. Only to crawl back to Aunt Lucinda's house on Juniper Avenue to wash himself and sober up so that Papa doesn't get too cross and withdraw his   allowance. Now he lounged in front of her, arm draped over his eyes to avoid the spring sunshine, and Ida   couldn't remember why she thought he and that boy from the exhibition – Clem – were anything alike.

'Master Daniel…'

'Oh, Daniel, my darling!'

Lucinda had appeared at the top of the stairs. She rushed to her nephew's side, skirts billowing, her face wracked with sympathy and reproach.

'Daniel, your father has been worried sick about you…'

'I know, I know,' Daniel moaned, waving his arm above his head. 'I am a wreck, a poor sailor on the sea of sudden sobriety. Though I have already been thoroughly reproached, dear Aunt, by the local constabulary.'

Lucinda gasped and smacked Daniel none too playfully around the head.

'You've been in trouble with the constables? Daniel, if your father finds out... I can't vouch for you when the law is involved, I always said –'

'Oh, it was nothing. There's this new Detective on the beat. Oakley? Oakden? Profoundly serious, very handsome, nice moustache. Barged into the – ahem, establishment – where I was – ahem, renting a room, and cleared us all out. Told him who I was, heir to the Loxport Express and all that. The rotter frog-marched me right out of there regardless and said next time it'd be a cell for me and dash it all who my father was. I felt very put out, I assure you.'

Oakden. Ida recognised the name. She'd never met the newest addition to the force, but she'd heard rumours from her buyers. Word was that this Detective had a passion for standards and a deep hatred for being shown up. He didn't sound like someone susceptible to flirting or name-dropping, Daniel's two main forms of conflict avoidance. But he was only one officer in a sea of lazy, ineffective lads with shiny badges and a love of strolling aimlessly. Not too much of a threat. Yet.

'But I'll be right as rain in a moment, and I'll be off to face my punishment from Papa. Ida here was just getting me a little breakfast, first…'

There was a sharp rap at the back door. Lucinda and Daniel looked to Ida. She sighed and went to answer it. She was going to the kitchen anyway, apparently.

Edith wasn't wearing her usual brown maid's uniform with the white apron and cap. She was wearing-

'Oh. Green. Um. Pretty?'

Edith looked down at her dress and laughed. The bodice was black and green vertical stripes, with a green lace skirt. It went with her hair, which somehow looked even redder and curlier than usual.

'It's canny, isn't it? I made it myself. I saved up for ages for the fabric, but I just had to have it.'

Her smile faded as she looked at Ida.

'You're…wearing your uniform to go out?'

What?

Oh.

Oh.

Between the new job and Daniel's interruption this morning, Ida had completely forgotten that Edith had strong-armed her into doing… something. Ida was about to say that there was a mix-up and that she had to work today, when Daniel wandered into the kitchen.

'Ida, where is my… oh. Hello.'

He leaned against the doorjamb, and all the hungover self-pity faded away. Edith was curvaceous, pretty, and fresh-faced; the kind of girl that men like Daniel wrote bad poetry about. He turned on his roguish, charming grin, and swept his curls from his eyes. That smile had turned both innocent ladies and upstanding young gentlemen into blushing, stammering idiots for more than six years. Edith didn't even blink.

'Good morning, sir,' she said, dipping into a curtsey. 'I've just come to collect Ida for our walk.'

'Walk?' Daniel asked, his features crumpling in confusion. Edith turned on her own sunny smile.

'Oh, yes – unless I have my days wrong? It is her day off today, Ms. Belmonte?'

Lucinda, who had appeared just behind Daniel, fluttered her hands in the girls' direction.

'Oh, of course. Edith, isn't it? From the Acutus?'

'Yes, ma'am.'

'Oh, wonderful, simply adorable! Yes, Ida, run along now with your little friend. I shall make Daniel his elevenses before he goes back to his Father's house in disgrace.'

Daniel's smile turned sickly. And was that a hint of a laugh in Lucinda's voice? Perhaps she was a little cannier to her nephew's pity parties than Ida thought.

'I'll go get my shoes, I suppose.'

Chapter Ten

———

'So,' Edith said, linking her arm through Ida's, 'where should we go?'

Ida had no idea. She had never been out socially in Loxport before.

'Um...'

'Well,' Edith interrupted, hugging Ida's forearm closer so she couldn't escape, 'I thought we could go to this cute little tearoom in the park. They do real cream scones with proper strawberry jam! My friend Beth works there, and she said she'd be expecting us.'

So why did you ask? Ida thought. But she simply nodded and allowed herself to be led.

Loxport had two parks: Calista Gardens, and Big Pond Park. Calista Gardens was where the wealthy and well-bred went to promenade aimlessly through perfectly maintained flower beds and blush at each other beside fountains and on park benches. Big Pond Park was actually called Albertian Plaza, but everyone called it Big Pond Park, because it had a big pond in it. It was a place where people let their children loose on the grass to play tag, where people laid out blankets on the ground to have a picnic, and where you could pull apples off the trees without expecting a hefty fine. In August you could go swimming, and every single year some idiot got arrested for trying to swim despite 'forgetting' his swimwear.

It turned out that near to the pond was a tiny tearoom called The Boathouse.

'It's actually where they used to put boats,' Edith explained as they walked, 'when you could go punting on the big pond. But they don't do that anymore – folks going out on the River Lox took all their business – so Bethany's boss saved the boathouse from being knocked down.'

Ida barely went into the parks. She had no time to. So, when Edith pushed open The Boathouse door, beaming, she had no idea what to expect.

It was cosy. Lace curtains, potted flowers on the sills that looked as if they had been excavated from the earth right outside the tearoom. The tables looked as if they had been salvaged from someone's living room (albeit someone with a smattering of taste: a comfortably well-off grandmother, perhaps), and winding between them was a rather portly tabby cat.

There was a girl behind the counter of about Edith's age. She lit up like the Schuyler Museum at night when she saw Edith, who immediately dragged Ida over to the counter.

'Edith! You made it back to see me.'

'I need one of those scones, Beth, with lots of jam. I've got the cravings.'

'Of course you have. I've got some still warm from the

oven, just for you.'

The girl – Beth – leaned on the counter, batting her eyelashes at Edith. This didn't surprise Ida in the slightest; she'd seen some of the other maids at the Acutus flirting with Edith from time to time. But that didn't stop Ida from feeling like a pony at a horseless stable. Again, Edith barely noticed her admirer.

'We'll have two please, Beth. With a pot of tea for the table. And how is my best friend? How is my handsome man? Oh, what a lovely gentleman you are, such a canny little laddie…'

What? Laddie? Oh. She was talking to the cat. While Edith tickled the tabby under the chin, Ida slipped her purse from the pocket sewn into her uniform. She did it with all her dresses for convenience. She had grabbed her purse and her shoes, but hadn't had time to change. The sooner she could get away from Daniel, the better.

'How much is that?'

Beth's gaze flicked to Ida for only a second, before looking back to Edith.

'Eight Athenas, please.'

'I could have paid for mine,' Edith said indignantly, the cat now in her arms. Ida shrugged.

'You've got your hands full.'

'I'll bring you another one of those chocolate bars from Mimi's. Did you like it?'

'I prefer sugared almonds.'

'Noted.'

They took a seat at a table near the window, and, in

between mouthfuls of scone, Edith talked, and Ida listened. Kate – the sister – was throwing a fit almost every morning at the moment because Edith had to work, and she didn't expect to be looking after a twelve year old at her age, and the Acutus was hiring out maids to do evening events at patrons' houses now, and it's good money but Kate would be on her own even more so she didn't know if she should she sign herself up… etc etc.

Edith clasped her hands around her teacup and looked Ida deep in the eyes. It made her uncomfortable.

'But that's not the reason I asked you here.'

She's found me out, Ida thought, somewhere deep in the back of her mind. She's confronting me, asking me to turn myself in…

'She's back.'

'Um. Yes. She is. It's…' Ida stirred another cube of sugar into her tea, buying for time, her mind scrambling for the correct answer. 'It's…good? It's bad.'

Edith's eyes burned into hers, until Ida finally gave up.

'Who's back?'

Edith smacked her on the arm, making her tea slosh in its cup.

'Who do you think? Blonde hair, fitted waistcoats, comes to the Acutus a lot when she's not out on a ship somewhere, the most gorgeous woman in the   entire flipping city?'

'Ah,' Ida said. She remembered now. 'The Scientist.'

'The Scientist!' Edith said, flinging her arms above her head in despair. 'She's back from her expedition, and she was at the club yesterday and she called me over to order and I still knew her order, Ida! Green tea with a lemon shortbread! She's been away for three months, and I interrupted her to repeat her order back! What am I going to do?!'

Odessa Malko, esteemed Cryptobiologist and Giver of Lectures At Exhibitions, was a regular at The Acutus Club. She'd fought a long battle to become one of its first female members and made the most of that privilege by taking a meal there at least once a week when she wasn't at sea. And she was the reason Edith never looked twice at anyone making romantic advances on her. She'd been smitten with the woman longer than Ida had known her, and talked about her with all the hand-wringing and angst you'd expect from a five Hermes romance pamphlet. She couldn't even use her real name without turning beetroot-red. And now she wanted advice on the matter? The last time Ida had any dealings with matters of the heart was when she was nine and she punched Luca Black for trying to kiss her.

'Well,' she attempted lamely, 'what can you do, eh?'

There was a long pause. Ida's stomach swirled anxiously. What else could she have said? It's not like Edith really wanted to be persuaded away from The Scientist…did she?

Did she?

'Exactly,' Edith groaned suddenly, swiping at the last of the jam on her plate with her finger. 'There's nothing I can do, is there? You're right, Ida: it's time to get over her. Who needs romance, anyway?'

'I agree. It's too confusing.'

Over Edith's shoulder, Ida noticed Beth disappear into the back room, crestfallen. Now would be a good time to swipe another scone for the trip home, she thought.

'You're the only love I need, aren't you Dougie?' Edith asked the cat, scooping him up in her arms again. 'Shall we go a-courting, eh? Shall we dance, my dearest?'

She leapt up and spun him around the room, singing some love song about dancing with your darling in the darkness, dancing with your love under the moo-oonlight. The cat looked less than thrilled. Edith's hair bounced around her head like coiled springs, and she threw her head back when she laughed. It must be odd, Ida thought, to show every thought you have on your face, all the time.

Dougie finally escaped Edith's clutches, and she finished her dance with a flourish, throwing her arms wide. Ida mimed applause, one eyebrow raised.

'Brava. So talented.'

'Should be on the stage, me.'

Edith plopped back down into her seat, out of breath and flushed.

'Thanks, Ida,' she said. 'You're a great listener.'

Ida's cheeks ached. She realised, on the walk back home, that it was because she'd been smiling.

Chapter Eleven

———

Ida and Edith walked back together through Loxport; Edith chattering away about whatever popped into her head, while Ida simply enjoyed being out in the fresh air. They were fast approaching Lucinda's home and frankly, she didn't want to go back yet. Loxport was a very   different city by day: very few ne'er do wells around. It was a lot nosier, too; Horselesses chuffing by, their wheels clattering, girls selling flowers and singing to each other, birds chirruping, dogs barking, people shouting greetings across the road…

'Ida? Ida!'

Ida blinked as Edith playfully shoved her shoulder.

'That sore a subject, is it?'

Oh, Lord. I wasn't listening.

'What?'

'I was asking you,' Edith sighed huffily, 'if your family drives you as wild as my Kate drives me. Honestly, was your tea laced with something stronger? You've gone all daydream-y.'

Ida's stomach turned cold. It was as if the word 'family' opened a door and let a wash of black water into her system. All the fun she had been having was swallowed up in it.

'Sorry. Yeah, my mam… my mam died. A while back.'

'Oh,' Edith's hand flew to her mouth. 'Ida, I'm so sorry.'

'It's fine,' Ida said automatically. It wasn't fine. At all. But it wasn't Edith's fault. She didn't know that Ida's mam was the only person who had ever believed in her and now she was gone and Ida had to manage all of this alone and the only person left was back on Tarnish Street and…

'Look,' Edith said, seizing her hand, 'does Lord Casterbury still call on your Lady?'

'Don't remind me –'

'Have I ever told you,' Edith said conspiratorially out of the corner of her mouth, 'about the time Lord Casterbury tried to romance an automaton?'

Something about that particular sentence shook Ida out of her trance. Perhaps it was the part about the person she hated most in the world trying to seduce what was essentially a useful statue.

'What?'

'Oh, Ida, let me tell you a tale!'

Edith spun Ida around with more strength than expected. Once their faces were close to each other, Edith continued.

'So. You know the bloke who makes those beautiful dancing girls – Mister McCorrell?'

'I think it's McConnell.'

'Whatever, he's not in the story for long. Anyway, he brought along this Automated Teasmaid to the Acutus one time, wondering if they wanted to invest. She was a beautiful thing, I have to say; really pretty face, tiny waist, obviously, and big blue eyes that looked like they were made of something expensive. They go off into the office to chat business. Of course, that thing'd take away all our jobs, so we were all pressed up behind the kitchen door, trying to listen in. Then Casterbury comes in, already stinking of opium before he even sits down… and he goes up to this maid – she's all kitted out in our uniform – and he asked her…'

Edith tried in vain to keep her voice level, but as her story continued, it rose into a high-pitched giggle of incredulity.

'He asked how such a pretty young thing came to be serving tea, and not to worry, he'll keep her safe from any ruffians that patronised the club! He was trying to get her name out of her when McConnell and the Acutus bosses came back out from the office.'

'No!'

'McConnell didn't even say anything, he just took back his Teasmaid and left!'

Ida's hand was clamped over her mouth.

'You. Are. Having. A. Laugh.'

'I am not! So, I should really go up to Mr. Casterbury one night and shake his hand. He's probably the reason I haven't been replaced with a metal girl!'

Edith was doubled over with laughter at her own story by this point. Her entire body seemed to shake with it. Ida's laugh was, by nature, a lot lower and softer, but even she couldn't quite wipe the grin from her face. How stupid. She knew what Edith was doing, of course. She didn't know what was more embarrassing: that she'd obviously needed cheering up, or that it had worked. 'Thanks for the mental image, Edith.'

'What are friends for? Now, off you trot: I have to go see what Kate's up to anyway. You want to do this again next week?'

Ida paused. This was probably a bad idea, but whatever. She'd had fun on her day off, for once, instead of just killing time after her pilgrimage to Tarnish Street, trying not to feel worse.

'We could. Maybe.'

Edith beamed, before turning on heel and striding off into the crowd. Ida took a deep breath, straightened out her expression, and entered the lion's den.

As Ida walked through the back door in the kitchen, she could see down the hallway to the front door. In between her and it, drifting down the stairs, was a myriad of dresses, scarves and petticoats, piling up in the middle of the floor. As Ida stepped over them, a headscarf drifted down like mist beside her. Someone was emptying Lucinda's wardrobe.

She slipped into her Rat Prince mindset almost immediately, as much as she could, given what she was wearing. Grabbing a fistful of her skirts in one hand to free up her movement, Ida cautiously crept up the stairs, silently emptying a vase and carrying it with her.

'…Ma'am?' Ida called, softly. 'Lucinda?'

Had someone worked out who she was? Had they

come looking for her stash of coins, and Lucinda had caught them in the act? If some little guttersnipe thought they could do this to The Damn Rat Prince, they'd have another thing coming...

'Ida? Ida, I need you.'

Lucinda sounded as if she'd been crying. Ida slowly pushed open her bedroom door, vase held aloft, ready to strike.

It looked as if a tornado had hit. Lucinda sat in the middle of her bedroom, alone. Every drawer, every wardrobe, every trinket box and every trunk had been opened and emptied on to the floor. Outfits, hats, artworks, jewellery; everything except for...

'I've lost the ruby brooch Devon bought for me.'

Lucinda sounded like a little girl waiting to be told off. Ida exhaled, placed the vase gently on the floor, amongst the rest of the detritus, and sat down next to her mistress.

'I'm... I'm sorry to hear that, ma'am. I check every item of clothing before it's washed, I haven't seen it.'

'Oh, I know you haven't lost it, Ida, dear,' Lucinda sniffed, wiping her tears on a pair of pantaloons that came to hand, 'I've lost it. I was so silly, I wanted to play some childish game with him to... what? Get more presents, more attention? As if I don't have enough. And he'll be so disappointed with me, and I hate disappointing people...'

Lucinda began to cry anew. Ida picked a spot on the floor at random and began to tidy.

'I'll keep a watch for it, ma'am. But I'm just glad you're safe. When I saw the house in disarray I thought I would need to call for a constable!'

Even if Lucinda had been lying in a pool of her own blood and the house had been set ablaze, Ida wouldn't call for the law enforcement of Loxport. She had a better chance of tracking down an attacker blindfolded with a broken leg.

'I'm sorry, Ida darling – is that why you had a vase? To bash an imaginary ruffian over the head?'

'I don't know if I have the strength, ma'am; I'd likely topple over from the weight of it!'

Lucinda tittered, wiping away her tears. As Ida began the task of folding, smoothing and re-hanging Lucinda's entire wardrobe, her mistress reached over to her bedside table and cupped an old, worn pocket watch, the style decades out of date, in her hands. Ida knew from polishing it a thousand times that the back was inscribed with the letters J.B.

'At least I didn't lose something important,' Lucinda whispered, so softly that Ida knew she wasn't meant to hear.

Chapter Twelve

During The Infamous Frog Incident, Ida had simply unscrewed the hinges on the museum's rooftop ventilation grate, shimmied down the heating pipes, and dropped herself onto the catwalk above the main rooms. Since then, the Schuyler had clearly learned their lesson. The grate now had a padlock on it. So scary.

A Carbrid triple-lock, to be fair; a big heavy thing that needed to be quickly picked three times in a row to allow entry. Enough to put off petty thieves in a rush and art-snobs whose closest brush with crime was being overcharged at La Niche for oysters. Ida was neither, and proud of it.

Ida had waited until the usual calls of goodnight and arrangements to meet at the pub had faded. Schuyler guards checked the roof exactly once, re-locked the Carbrid, then focused on making sure the front door was secure and the year-round exhibits were where they should be. Then they spent the rest of their shift sitting on their backsides in the foyer. Ida had made her way to the rooftop, settled in and watched the night sky darken overhead as she waited for the museum below her to quieten. The kittiwakes were coming back to Loxport for the warmer months, and Ida listened to their half-melodic cries with a fond nostalgia. Her mam used to take her down to the ports to watch the kittiwakes feeding their babies, flying back to nests perched high up on scaffolding and window ledges. 'The higher you go,' her mam told her, 'the safer you are.' Time to get to work.

Lockpicking, for Ida, was a way to relax. Her mind could focus when she was picturing pins and springs in a way that didn't happen when she was busying herself with dusting or mopping. It felt right. Like this was what she was meant to be doing.

It was around one in the morning when she gently pried the grate away and began her decent into the museum. Once she was inside it was cool, dark, and quiet. The phosphorus light fixtures were turned down for the night, tiny blue particles settling near the bottom of the lamps like sand. From her position on the catwalk Ida felt as though she were looking down into deep, dark water, full of sea creatures. She climbed to a place where she could descend into the corridors of the Schuyler safely, then crept to the front of the museum; past the crypto-biology wing, past Dirigibles Through History, and past the commemorative statue of King Albert I – pioneer of technology and the advancement of the Scientific Arts. He was the man who saw the potential in the coal-rich North of England and, over his reign, turned it into a bustling hive of innovation, art and science. In his arms was Princess Victoria the Second, now about Ida's age, and never seen publicly.

Ida knew from overhearing snatches of conversation that all the eligible bachelors of Loxport were just dying to know when her debut would be. Purely with a patriotic mindset, of course.

In front of the Royal Family was the foyer. To either side were wings that Ida knew from her previous casing of the museum were used for storage. Ida could hear the guards – two of them, both men – discussing some boating tournament that was happening at the weekend. She picked a door at random and, as the guards roared with laughter at some inane joke, crept towards it, lockpicks in hand.

Over the next ten minutes she eased the door open, painfully slowly. Yes, this was where the stuff for the outdoor exhibition was being kept overnight.

Let's see, Ida thought. There's that dancing girl, the camera spiritus, a zoetrope of Loxport Through Time… no gems. Damn it. That means…

It meant she had to creep over to the other wing and spend more precious minutes opening that door. Sure enough, Clem's leather trunk was there, underneath some papers about more efficient velocipedes. The padlock was probably older than Ida was. Less than a minute later, the green gem was in her pocket, and she was easing the door shut again. Then back over to the other wing, for her distraction.

'It all depends on the conditions, Greg – the conditions!'

'Nah, nah, mate, Oliver's gonna smash that record, you'll see. He's been training for…'

So-So-So-So let me d-d-dance you my deeeevotion.
Fffor I have no words at all…

'Ah, hell, the bloody machine's gone off again.'

'Hang on, hang on, you needy wench, we're coming!'

'Bring a bloody hammer, Tom, ha ha.'

'More than my job's worth, you tit.'

Ida was already running silently towards the catwalk, the gem bumping against her knee, deep in her pocket.

'Aw, Greg man, did you not shut the door properly?'

'Coulda sworn I did…the other one's locked, though? Gawd, sorry Tom, I'd forget my head if it wasn't screwed on.'

'It's ok, Greg. I still love you.'

'…love you too, mate.'

As the automaton was finally quietened, Ida was hanging from the opening in the roof, swinging her legs up underneath her. Once, twice, three times and she was up, scrabbling for purchase on the concrete outside. Just got to get the grate back on; quietly, quietly… Done. She was out.

Ida backed up against the lip of the roof to catch her breath for a second before starting her trip back to the chosen cubby hole. She had to hide the gem for a day or two, let the heat die down before contacting Casterbury. And that would be its own kettle of fish.

But for now, she thought, as she fished the gem from her pocket and flourished it, triumphantly, just above eye level, it was another job well done for The Rat –

Her vision exploded.

Chapter Thirteen

―――――

Green light covered the gem, Ida's hands, and the entirety of her feet. The stone was also now excreting a thick, glowing foam that felt absolutely disgusting as it slid over Ida's skin. She swallowed a cry of shock as the gem shot out of her hands, rattling along the rooftop, banging loudly against the Carbrid lock. Her shadow was thrown out behind her as the light flashed up into the sky. Ida didn't have time to think. She threw herself on top of the gemstone, covering it up with her body as she stuffed it under her tunic. She curled around it like a woodlouse, tucking her head against her chest, barely noticing that, despite all the light it was omitting, the gemstone wasn't hot. The only thing she could do is silently beg it to stop, please, please stop whatever the bloody hell it is your doing so I can finish stealing you!

She stayed like that for an horrific few minutes, watching the greenish shadows shrink back along the concrete lip of the rooftop inches from her face. She could feel the soapy foam soaking her tunic and the gem thumping against her ribs. Slowly – far too slowly for Ida's liking – the last of the light faded away, and everything was still. Ida finally allowed herself to peek over the edge of the roof. No one had seen her. Hopefully.

Ida slowly rolled over into a sitting position and extracted the gem from her tunic carefully, as though it were a live snake.

'What the hell was that?' she whispered.

The gemstone lay in her hand, cool and still. In the newly fallen darkness, she couldn't see the gradient from bright to gentle green.

Alright, Rat Prince, let's think about this logically, shall we? What changed between taking this thing out of Clem's trunk, where it was behaving itself, and just now, when it went off in my hand? Well, it was in my pocket as I ran though the museum, and climbed the ladder, and then I took it out and shook it like an idiot…

Was it the movement? Had she somehow activated it with the shaking? That was going to make it very difficult to get back home. And she had to move soon; there was always a chance the guards decided to check on the commotion she had caused.

Right then. Move quickly, move smoothly, and take breaks after each jump. And don't get caught. Simple enough.

Keeping her hand clamped to her pocket, Ida began the long journey back to Juniper Avenue. She climbed back in through her window at about four in the morning, far later than she'd imagined when she plotted her route back. Bracing upon impact on every rooftop and pausing while hanging from every drainpipe to check she didn't have a frothing, rattling lantern in her pocket had doubled the time it had taken, not to mention the fact that climbing one-handed had knackered her sense of balance. She could have just under two hours of sleep before she was expected to be awake and working. Her clothes were clinging to her stomach, soaked from the foam. She was freezing and tired, and wondering why nothing to do with Devon pissing Casterbury ever went smoothly. She closed her window behind her, tucked the green rod securely between the coffee cans and box of practice locks in her wardrobe, and was asleep before her head hit the pillow. Her dreams enclosed her like a thick, dark shroud. And out of that shroud came shapes, fuzzy at first, growing clearer and realer, all tinged a sickly, wrong colour.

Midnight. I fly over rooftops made of sugar. My footsteps sing, the stars above like diamonds on cool, black silk. Ripe for taking. The moon, white as a bone. As a death.

'Ida?'

Somewhere below me, my mother pleads.

'Come back. Save me. Ida!'

Fingers stretch, joints pop; hands barely touch. She is cold. The moon turns. It's sick now, wrong, drooling bubbling green sludge. Cobblestones are spattered, spat on, the city flooded. Consumed, drowned…

'Ida!'

I slip. Plummet with sickening, shattering speed, back to the gutter. Where I belong.

'Mam!'

She started upright in her bed as if she were spring-loaded. In the hallway, Lucinda tapped on the door, as light as rain.

'Ida, darling, are you alright? Did I hear you… crying?'

Ida wiped her face. She must have been sweating bullets. Her whole face was damp.

'Um…'

'Do you need a doctor, dear?'

The door handle squeaked as Lucinda tried to open it, not knowing that Ida had secured a bolt on the other side. Ida flung her hand out to stop her all the same.

'No! No, ma'am, it's alright. Just a… just a nightmare. I'm sorry to wake you.'

A pause.

'If you're sure, dear… you know where I am if I need to call for the doctor.'

'I'm fine, ma'am. Thank you.'

Lucinda's footsteps faded away down the hall, back to her room. Ida listened for the soft click of her own bedroom door closing, then snatched up a pillow and hugged it as tight as she could. She took a few gulping deep breaths, taking in the scent of her worn cotton pillowcase and her macassar hair oil, squeezing her eyes shut, hoping the iridescent colours that swirled over her vision would replace the memory of her mother's face. It didn't work. It never did.

Chapter Fourteen

———

Molly Finn hadn't been a great beauty. She had a voice like a gurgling drainpipe, and she knew nothing of poetry or politics. But by God, she was smart, and she was quick. She could put a price to every item in a tavern with one glance and be halfway down the street with the most valuable trinket in her pocket before you realised she was gone. She could out-talk, out-think, and outrun any man Ida had ever met. If she'd been born into a family like Lucinda's, with all her influence and money, she could've ruled the world. Instead, she'd started Ida pickpocketing at five, taught her how to hide her accent by seven, and had her installed as a maid by twelve.

'You won't end up in the gutter, hinny,' she'd told her. 'No daughter of mine is gonna spend her life eating scraps.'

She would have approved of Lucinda as a disguise. Silly, sweet, and helpless without good old Ida to keep her company. But her plan to evict Casterbury from their lives would have been a thousand times more elegant, and probably resolved by now. They'd probably have laughed about it.

Ida missed her every single day.

The next morning, Lucinda gave Ida a horrifically

pitying look as she descended the stairs for breakfast. The dreams had returned as soon as Ida had closed her eyes again so, in the end, she stayed awake; flipping through the pages of a pamphlet and forgetting what she'd read by the time she turned the page. She had managed to get all of her chores done for the morning, but now her vision was blurry and her head felt like a ton weight. Lucinda cupped her cheek, and Ida was too tired to protest, even internally.

'Poor dear,' Lucinda tutted. 'Clear the dishes, then have a little sleep. Come back to your chores later. I'll take my lunch at the Casterbury Emporium.'

'Ma'am…' Ida protested, embarrassed. Lucinda waggled her finger.

'No, no. They have a new tea-room on the third floor I have been meaning to try. They serve their crumpets with boysenberry conserve all the way from the Americas!'

She grinned, all sunny innocence, and something twinged in Ida's chest. She was grateful. Lucinda had done something selfless. How odd. Ida could hear her mother laughing: Don't look a gift horse in the mouth.

Ida nodded mutely, and waited in the wings to clear away the dishes before slinking away to her quarters, defeated and exhausted and ready to let sleep take her.

Sugar-topped shingles turn sickly-sweet and cloying. Rot your teeth. The city's rotting, the skyline tumbles into a waiting, hungry sea and you are small, so easy to wash away in this city's riptide. Run away, hinny. Don't trip on the cobbles of Tarnish Street. If you do

You will fall and fall

And fall and fall and –

Fall.

Ida lurched awake again.

This felt unfair. Spiteful, somehow, on behalf of her brain. She'd had a really, really long night, and she couldn't even escape for an hour or two into a nap; a Lucinda-approved nap, at that. She couldn't be getting too old for the adrenaline rush of a near-escape already, surely? She wasn't even twenty.

She'd dreamt of her mother before. Many times. But these dreams seemed like something altogether different. They were distorted. Sick. Tinged with something wrong.

Forget it. If she had the house to herself, she intended to do some research.

Ida got up and sat cross-legged on her bedroom floor, gem in her hands. This thing had erupted after a daring dash through the museum. So, what would happen if…

She shook it from side to side, as gently as she could. Nothing. She waggled it briskly in the air like a magic wand. Some inner core began to flare up, the glow weaker in the light of a sunny Loxport afternoon, but still visible. She rolled it across the floor with a flick of her hand for added speed, and the glow intensified. It came to a stop, caught on a loose floorboard, and then, after a second, rattled where it sat. Ida watched as the rod spun in a brisk circle, pale green light shimmering up the walls like an aurora. A snail's-trail of bubbly, green sludge seeped into the wood. As Ida grabbed one of her dirty dresses to mop it up, she contemplated the still spinning gem, caught as it was on the floorboard.

'What on earth have you bought, Casterbury?' she wondered aloud.

Night rolled around again, and The Rat Prince pulled on his goggles and set out. Beyond curiosity and safety measures – Ida took a route to her drop-off spot that included minimal leaps – there was no reason to wonder too deeply on what this particular treasure was for. Money was money. And besides, Casterbury could possibly blow himself up with it, which was a plus.

Casterbury apparently didn't know where the Lord and Horse was, so they had arranged to meet in the Industrial Estates. The Rat Prince did not make trades in the affluent parts of the city. She loitered on a rooftop, lit by the oily orange light of a streetlamp, until she saw his tall, bulky shape moving from streetlamp to streetlamp. She moved into position in the shipyard itself, hidden by the mist from the sea.

Far off, at the beginnings of the Scientific Estates, the Loxport Bridge curved over the river like a wishbone. They were going to install bio-luminescence into it soon, so it would light up at night, shimmering over the water. Ida thought it would just look like the dome of a giant jellyfish, come to destroy the city. Somewhere behind her, the muffled roar of a crowded pub drifted on the wind, and overhead, the kittiwakes sang to her. The tang of salt air tingled her nose. That was what she loved about   living in the North. Not the showy, fancy stuff. The smell of salt air, laughter in the distance, and birds flying towards the sea. Towards freedom.

As Casterbury moved closer, Ida slipped into place, watching him walk with what he obviously assumed was a hard bloke's swagger. He was clearly enjoying his little foray into the murkier side of Loxport; he'd even come incognito. Oh, for God's sake.

'Is that you, Casterbury?' The Rat Prince purred from atop a massive coil of chain, waiting to be attached to some anchor and plunged into the freezing ocean. 'I didn't recognise you under that masterful disguise.'

Devon Casterbury pulled the bakers-boy hat down as far as it would go. It was too small for him. Had he borrowed it from one of his stable boys? What a tit.

'Let's just get this over with,' he muttered into the collar of his coat.

'I'm sorry?' The Rat Prince said, standing and swiping imaginary dust from his tunic, enjoying the excuse for theatricality. 'What was that? You don't want this little trinket anymore? No bother, I have another buyer lined up for tomorrow night–'

'No!' Casterbury spluttered, before covering it up with a discreet cough. 'I mean… let's get the wages settled, shall we?'

'I don't take a wage, mate. I'm what they call an independent contractor. Leave the money at the foot of the chain, then you head into that alley across the road and count to two hundred. When you come back to admire the view, you'll have your trinket.'

As Casterbury tucked the money behind a huge bin of waste scraps of metal, The Rat Prince examined his fingernails, the mist off the Lox turning sickly orange around him.

'So,' he said, almost to himself, 'you out to impress someone with that thing? You might get more than you bargained for, mate.'

Casterbury smirked up at him through the fog. It was a sly, smug smile that ached to be punched right off his face.

'I certainly hope so, "mate".'

Ooh, cocky Casterbury.

The Rat Prince slid into a crouch, high above Casterbury's head. He tilted his head, animal-like, and his green eyes glinted wickedly above his widening smile.

'I'd be on my way soon, Casterbury. This isn't a savory place for a man of your... stature.'

A less honorable thief would have had three of Loxport's hardest waiting in that alley to relieve Casterbury of anything valuable he had on him. But instead he emerged a moment or two later, safe and sound and bee-lining towards a small package wrapped in brown paper, tucked under a streetlamp. Had Ida not been so sick and tired then, maybe she wouldn't ensure that Casterbury would be watching his back all the way to his cosy townhouse in Innovation Court. She wouldn't make the darker parts of the city seem like hiding places for a phantom nor would she make shadows flit over his head as he walked through his expensive neighbourhood, or take a horrible, vicious joy in watching Casterbury look over his shoulder every other step, sure that something was watching him. Or that the very same something wouldn't scrape its lockpicking kit over his window about an hour after he extinguished his light, sending a blood-chilling noise resonating throughout Casterbury's house and into his mind, rocketing him out of bed with a cry. But a Prince has to have his fun, after all.

Chapter Fifteen

———

Ida was still tired the next morning. Yet more sickly, off-kilter dreams had plagued her in the night. Fewer of them, yes, but no less potent or spiteful. Her mother's face, tinged in sickly-coloured light, still swam in front of her eyes as she stretched. Perhaps she shouldn't have sacrificed another night of sleep for a petty bit of schadenfreude. But it was worth it. Those two thousand Athenas were sitting snugly in their cans in the wardrobe, and she'd climbed into bed with Casterbury's startled yaps of surprise keeping her company well into the wee hours.

Lucinda was still wracked with guilt over 'losing' her brooch. On Friday, the day of her invitation to dinner and the opera with Dear Devon, she was practically manic with unspent energy.

'Ida, what am I going to say?' she said, pacing the drawing room floor while Ida tried to sweep. 'What if he co-ordinates his outfit with the brooch? What if he shouts at me? What if he doesn't want to see me again, and I become a mad old widow, all alone with, with… fifteen parrots?'

'It was an accident, ma'am,' Ida countered, abandoning the sweeping and taking up her feather duster. 'Lord

Casterbury seems an empathetic man. He'll understand. If not, I'll arrange a contractor to put up an aviary in the garden.'

'Don't tease me, Ida,' Lucinda said flopping into a chair, skirts billowing up almost to her chin. 'Besides, if I am to be an eccentric in my old age, the parrots would have to be inside the house. I'd name them after famous inventors, and I'd teach them to sing ' "Land of Hope And Industry."' She waved her hands in the air, conducting an imaginary orchestra. '"Da da da-da-da dum dummm, pride in brilliancy…" Squawk!'

Ida laughed. She had to admit it; Lucinda could be funny, underneath all that pomp.

You're more tired than you thought. You're letting your guard down.

'I know,' Lucinda exclaimed from her seat, 'let's go out into Loxport. Fresh air, that's the tonic. I want to go back to the Schuyler exhibition. I wonder if that sweet boy Clem will be there again. Go get dressed, Ida.'

…fine.

The exhibition wasn't quite as crowded as the opening day, but crowds still milled from stall to stall, congregating to chat by the fountain. After a few moments of idly glancing at other exhibitors, Lucinda flapped her hand excitedly in greeting.

'Yoo-hoo! Clem, dear! Do you remember me?'

Clem was staring off into space as Lucinda and Ida approached, but he snapped to attention as he heard his name being called.

'Oh! My favourite patron! How are you faring today, Madam?'

On the walk over, Ida had noticed that Lucinda had slipped the Bismuth necklace around her neck that morning. As she approached the stall it caught the late morning sunshine, glittering attractively. Clem gestured to it, hand on heart, as if he'd been shot with an arrow.

'And you're wearing the Bismuth! I couldn't ask for a more glamorous endorsement of my humble wares, Ms. Belmonte.'

As he spoke, Clem caught Ida's eye and smiled; barely a flicker of the lips, but it was there, nonetheless. When he smiled, the drama and the showmanship didn't fade away exactly, they just became a little more real. Ida kept her face straight, while Lucinda simpered. But her cheeks warmed, just a touch.

'Oh, Clem, they are anything but humble! I have had nothing but compliments on your designs since we were here last; have I, Ida, dear?'

'No, ma'am.'

'And I was wondering if you had anything new that I could snap up for a special event tonight?'

Ida blinked. What was this, now? Not only losing Casterbury's brooch, but wearing something made by the boy who embarrassed him a few days ago? Lucinda belonged to a social class that sent messages with flowers. Didn't she see how this could go?

Clem spread his hands wide in apology. Something in his face looked genuinely sad, not performatively guilty or regretful. If Ida was a lesser thief, she would have felt her cheeks truly redden.

'I'm sorry, Madam, I really am. I had a…' Clem coughed discreetly, 'misfortune earlier in the week, and I haven't been back in my smithy since. If you come back later in the exhibition, though?'

'Oh, Clem darling. I hope it's nothing too serious?'

'Well, no one is hurt, I suppose. I'm just professionally disheartened. Thank you, for your support, Ms. Belmonte.'

They were clasping hands now. Lucinda drew back after a moment to dab at her eyes with a handkerchief.

'Ida… pick something.'

'What?' Ida exclaimed, stepping backwards before she could stop herself. Lucinda nodded.

'You've worked so hard recently, and been so tired, bless your soul. And Clem is in need. Pick something out for yourself. It can be an early birthday present.'

'Ma'am…

'Ida, I'm not asking.'

A little steel entered Lucinda's voice as she spoke. Clem's gaze slid to meet Ida's, and he broke out into a slow, wide grin. Ida hated this boy so much, she almost laughed.

'Welcome,' he almost shouted, 'to my humble stall, Miss…um…'

'Finn,' Lucinda stage-whispered, enjoying the game now, 'her last name is Finn.'

'Miss Finn! Can I interest you in some simply gorgeous

garnet, set on a fine copper chain that would go wonderfully with your complexion? Or perhaps these Purple Lepsum earrings, a one-of-a-kind set…'

In the end, Ida was cajoled, flattered and bullied into picking out a simple pearl on a black ribbon. 'It would sit nicely under my uniform,' she reasoned, as Clem slipped it into a small drawstring bag for her. The real reason was that it didn't cost a lot. As Lucinda said her goodbyes, Clem asked if she could spare Ida to chat, just for a moment. Lucinda giggled at Ida before flouncing off into the crowd to look at the Black Shuck puppy again. As soon as she was lost to the throng, Clem leaned in close.

'Her suitor. That Casterbury bloke. Are they a dead cert for marriage?'

Ida stared at him sardonically.

'Why? Think you've got a chance?'

Clem snorted a laugh.

'Probably. But no.'

Clem grasped Ida's hand and yanked her across the table so he could murmur in her ear.

'Get off me, you absolute –'

'That gemstone I was saving to be examined? Gone. Stolen. And I think I know who arranged it.'

Ida's blood ran cold. Every muscle in her face strived to remain as relaxed as possible as she asked; 'You know that for certain?'

'Pretty much. Jealous old man kicks up a stink, a few days later it's gone?' Clem grinned, 'Luckily, I have a few underworld contacts of my own. That Casterbury better start double and triple-locking his doors, 'cos the guy I'm looking to hire doesn't cut corners when it comes to burglary. He's infamous, he is. A Crown Prince of Criminality, you could say.'

Ida's veins were frozen solid. She took a deep breath, and clasped Clem's arm.

'If I hear anything, I'll get back to you.'

The smile softened, turned grateful and – thank God – trusting.

'Thanks, Ida. You're a gem, no pun intended. Us little people gotta look out for each other, eh?'

He leaned across the table, and his eyes met hers.

'And I hope you don't mind me saying that the pearl suits you. It really does. No hyperbole, no sales pitch. You don't need anything flash.'

Ida felt that warmth on her face again. Not a proper blush, obviously. Just a spot of colour on each cheekbone.

Odd. Very, very odd. '…thanks, Clem.'

'My pleasure, Miss Finn.'

After she said her goodbyes and turned away, Ida allowed herself half a second to rub her eyelids, pinch her nose tightly, and groan.

She almost didn't have to check her cubby holes that night. She already knew what she'd find there.

Chapter Sixteen

——

If Casterbury reported the theft to the constables, he would be putting his foot in it; he'd have to admit how he came across the item that had been stolen in the first place. But Casterbury didn't have the sense to realise that. And even if he did, he had more than enough money to bribe someone on the beat to let this little indiscretion go. This Detective Oakden may have morals, but he couldn't be assigned to every case. Oh, God. She'd followed him home that night. She'd been at his house. The temptation to put the frighteners up Casterbury had been too much to ignore. All Casterbury would have had to do was fling open his curtains and he would have seen her, crouched on his window like some kind of gargoyle. What if his neighbours were out for a midnight stroll? Stupid, arrogant, petty girl that she was. This is what happens when you get involved, Ida…

No. No, she couldn't do it. She was turning the job down.

She hated turning a job down. It was bad for business. And bad for money. Clem wasn't offering as much as Casterbury had, but Ida suspected it was most of his earnings from the exhibition. But she'd have to roll with the loss, this time.

Clem was meeting her behind The Lord and Horse for her answer. It was Sunday, and that meant most of the patrons had lost their rowdy, it's-the-weekend energy and become a healthy cocktail of tired, sad and partially hungover. Nice and lethargic, less likely to pick up on her presence. She perched herself on the same stable wall she'd used to seal her deal with Reg. God, she was getting tired. She had spent her entire weekend agonising over whether she was going to take the job or not, knowing full well the entire time that she wasn't. She kept thinking about the old coffee cans of money in her wardrobe, about her next trip down to Tarnish Street, about the guilt sloshing about in her stomach, about the note that had been tied to the kitchen door this morning that said See you Wednesday! E. xx. About how in the space of a week she had enjoyed being around Lucinda, been on a day out with Edith, and how she'd also jeopardised her foothold in Loxport's criminal community.

A rock rattled down the alleyway, kicked by a wary, hesitating, gangly shape at the entrance that manifested itself into Clem. He walked down the cobblestones, pulling up the collar of his greatcoat around his ears. Ida collected herself.

'You Clem?'

The voice at the end of the alley was soft and raspy, but it carried. Clem tried not to jump as the fabled green eyes shimmered in the dark. He cleared his throat.

'Yes.' He shoved his hands into his pockets, attempting to swagger. 'Why don't you step into the light, Mr. Rat

Prince? I might like what I see…'

'I'm not really in the mood,' snapped the reply. 'Look, I'm not doing the job, mate. I'm sorry. I'm double-booked.'

Clem's face dropped.

'W-what? You…can't do it?'

'Not can't. Won't. Will not.'

Clem stepped forward. When he spoke, his voice broke. 'I… wh… look, if it's a money thing…'

A click, a swish, and the shimmer of a blade appeared at The Rat Prince's thigh.

'I wouldn't come closer.'

Clem froze in place. Slowly, his expression curdled from surprise and more than a little fear into indignation.

'Some master thief you are. What's the matter, Rat Prince? Scared to go up against one of the elite?'

The knife whistled through the air and landed with a thwock at Clem's feet. He looked up at The Rat Prince's silhouette and snorted.

'Yeah, aye. Whatever,' Clem muttered as he turned on his heel and stormed away into the Loxport evening. As he approached the alleyway entrance, he paused for a moment. His shoulders hitched – just once – and the forearm of his coat passed over his eyes in one angry swipe. And then he was gone. Ida waited fifteen minutes before slinking down to the cobbles to retrieve her knife. She'd done the right thing. She was safe. A person she barely knew was inconvenienced in the process. She could live with that.

So why did she feel so awful?

Chapter Seventeen

———

'Ida!'

The delicate tinkle of a china cup falling to the floor was enough to bring Lucinda barrelling into the kitchen. Ida was staring at the pieces of broken pottery with a blank expression, as if she wasn't entirely sure how they got there. Lucinda rolled her eyes.

'Honestly, what is the matter with you this week? Weeping spells, tiredness, and now clumsiness?'

'Sorry, ma'am,' Ida muttered dully, 'I'll go get the broom.'

'At least it wasn't a MacNeal original,' Lucinda conceded. 'I'd be devastated if you broke one of those.'

Ida thought of the delicate butterfly-patterned saucer that languished somewhere in the compost heap and kept her mouth shut. This was not her week. Casterbury hadn't even brought up the subject of the lost brooch with Lucinda, just smiled and tapped her on the nose like a naughty kitten, then started bloviating about some   project he had in mind.

Only one more day until some time off. She planned on doing nothing – or as little of nothing as she could get away with – all day. She still had to go down to Tarnish Street. And all that entailed. And she'd have to practice her lock-picking, or she'd get sloppy. And do her stretches in the morning. But then, sleeping all day. That sounded ideal.

'Your penance,' Lucinda announced, presenting Ida with a lilac envelope, sealed with violet wax, 'is an errand to Sixpence Street to deliver this note to Clem.'

Really? When had Ida's life become so convoluted? Well, she supposed that it was better than drying (and breaking) more dishes. Sixpence Street was right on the edge of the Industrial Estates; as close to the ports and the shipyards as you could get without being a boat. Not far from where The Rat Prince had closed the sale with Casterbury, actually. Ida enjoyed the walk. The rambling, cobbled backstreets with their terraced houses and shops, each with their own walled-in back yard and tiny coal shed, reminded her of her childhood. And the best part? After she was done being nostalgic, she got to leave.

Clem's smithy was perched on the end of Sixpence Street. The storefront's paint was a little faded, but the sign itself was fresh and bright: snow-white lettering on a navy background that cheerily announced itself as Clem Magnesan, Gemologist: Custom Jewellery and Gemstones of the Highest Quality. A battered old velocipede rested against the wall. At least it looked more upstanding than the lewd pottery shop. Ida rapped on the door, and a dishevelled, slightly red in the face Clem opened the door.

'Oh! Ida!' he beamed, wiping his brow with a slightly

off-white sleeve. 'Come in, come in, you're letting all the hot air out.'

Ida waved the envelope in his face.

'I'm just here to deliver a note from Lucinda.'

'I know, I know,' Clem winked from under his fringe as he wiped a sheen of sweat from his brow, 'but you'd be ever so rude if you didn't come in for a cup of tea, while you're here. Plus, who doesn't like a good skive from work?'

Admittedly, he had a point.

Clem's smithy was a room of two parts, separated by an archway of large red bricks. The front half was occupied by a bench made of dark wood, glass cases filled with jewellery and boxes of raw gems. On the desk was a mannequin's head, showing off a matching necklace and earring set, and on the table was a glass bowl filled with tiny, smooth beads for watches and gadgets that Ida longed to plunge her hand into. Beyond the red wall was a disaster. A fire blazed in the forge, casting orange light onto the various sheets of copper and iron and racks of metal tools that lined the walls. And lay on the workbenches. And the floor. Clem saw Ida's expression, and laughed.

'I would've tidied up if I knew I was getting company today. I'll bring you a drink, if you let me finish what I'm doing. Take a seat; there's a little chaise in the shop.'

So there was, a worn leather thing that looked like it came from someone's jumble sale, tucked into a corner by the window. It was the most comfortable thing Ida had ever sat on. She had thirty seconds of luxuriating in the worn cushions and warm leather smell before she found herself fiddling with the envelope in her hand, trying not to be nosy about her surroundings. She reckoned she could break into this place without even bringing her lockpicks. The hinges on the windows and the door looked as if a stiff breeze would cause them to disintegrate. Just take the stuff from the front of the store, no need to rifle through all the blacksmithing tools unless someone had requested them…

A metallic bang snapped Ida out of her thoughts. Clem was back at his forge, a red-hot piece of metal balanced on his anvil. He grabbed a hammer, flipped it one-handed into his palm, and began striking at the metal, flattening it into a long, smooth rectangle. His strawberry-blond hair, damp with sweat, fell over his right eye, and he stuck out his lower lip and blew it away with a puff of air.

He'd always looked tall and thin, but as he worked with the metal Ida could see that what she'd taken for lankiness was actually lithe and toned: the sleeves of his shirt were rolled up to the elbow (for all the good it did to keep them out the way, they were still smudged with smoke and sweat), and the muscles of his forearms stood out as he hit the hammer against the anvil.

His skin was dusted with freckles, surprisingly fine hair and tiny, old scars. A bead of sweat ran down his neck and disappeared under the collar of his shirt.

Ida suddenly found her mouth very dry.

After an agonising five minutes, Clem plunged the metal into a barrel of water and looked up to find Ida staring.

'Y'alright, Ida?'

'Yes!' Ida squawked, sitting even more upright than she had been. 'Just… not sleeping well. Staring into space, you know.'

'Aye, insomnia is a blight on the human race, isn't it?' Clem winced in sympathy. 'Had some not very long ago myself. I'll get you some water – not from this barrel, mind! The fresh stuff, just for prestigious guests. Nice and cold, it'll perk you right up.'

He busied himself somewhere in the back, then plonked himself down next to Ida with two clay mugs of delicious, cold water.

'A mate of mine rigged me up a bootleg Ice-Chest,' he explained as Ida gulped her drink down. 'Made it out of old pipes and a beaten-up Automaton fan, essentially. Doesn't have the perpetual ice generator at the back, but it works just the same as a fancy one from the Emporium. So,' he stretched, scratching the damp nape of his neck, 'what's her Ladyship after this time?'

'I thought you liked Lucinda?' Ida asked.

'Oh, I do. She seems very sweet. But she's also a bit…' Clem fluttered his hands by his cheeks in a perfect impersonation. '"Oh, jolly good, Clem darling! Pip pip!" You know?'

Ida laughed. She did know. 'I think she's commissioning you,' she said, handing over the envelope, 'she does love a good sob story.'

'It wasn't a sob story,' Clem replied. 'This is the first time I've been back in the smithy for a week. I've really missed it, but I couldn't work after the theft, I was so   gutted.'

'But you didn't even know what the gem was. It could be just a pretty piece of glass,' Ida lied.

'But it's not just about the gem, is it?' Clem's gaze was distant as he looked back into the chaos of his smithy. 'I've fought really hard to be the person I am,' he sighed, 'to have the freedom to be the real me, and to have what I have. And some entitled, spoiled tosser with too much money and a bruised ego feels he can take a piece of that just because… what? Because I'm smarter than him, more talented than him, certainly more handsome than him. And I dare to do all of that while being poor, and being a smart-arse, and being…'

Clem waved a hand by his face in a vague gesture.

'…me. So, where's my chance to excel? I don't get one, apparently. 'You could have stumbled onto something expensive, something special – or at least something pretty to inspire your next work – but you don't get to keep it, my son."

Ida had never been around a client – or a victim – after a job. She didn't exactly run in the same circles as a lot of her victims; if she was ever at a garden party, she was there to serve the drinks. And she had barely ever socialised with anyone with a background like hers. Between Edith and this boy, Ida suddenly felt as if she were being dragged, kicking and screaming, into having friends. Which made the previous night sting all the harder.

Clem shook his head, and a droplet of sweat fell from his hair and landed on his forearm. 'Sorry. You don't care about this, I'm just waffling.'

'I didn't say that.'

Clem nodded. Then he took back her mug. His fingertips brushed against her knuckles.

'I've kept you too long. Lucinda will need her banisters dusting or something.'

'Don't joke. You haven't seen the house yet. That takes a long while.'

'Well perhaps when I come to drop off her commission,' Clem said, meeting her gaze, 'I can stay for tea.'

'Perhaps.' The moment lingered for a second longer than Ida expected.

'Come on,' Clem said, flinging his arms wide. 'I bared my soul to you, Ida Finn. I think we're on a hugging basis now.'

Nope. Ida did not trust herself enough for that. Not yet, and possibly not ever. They settled on a handshake. Clem's fingers were long, and slender, but he shook her hand with a briskness she didn't expect. His palm was warm.

Ida had said her goodbyes, closed the door behind her and walked halfway back to Juniper Avenue before she caught herself smiling.

Oh, get a grip, girl. This is becoming a habit.

Chapter Eighteen

———

Ida needed a distraction. A simple, easy job with no stakes, no baggage. And she knew just the one to take.

The Eshneal Building was a short, squat building at the very edge of the Industrial Estate; just before the road turned a corner and became blue-tinged and fashionable. It was a place where writers and artists, poets and mavericks, came together to sit on the floor, smoke cheap Opium, and talk about revolution without straying too far into the darker, dirtier parts of Loxport. Education and employment for all! Then a ten-minute Brightwind ride back to Daddy's winter lodgings for sherry – how jolly! One of the Rat Prince's contacts – for only a select few knew exactly how to contact him – had relayed a message from one of these sensitive little souls. Apparently the Eshneal was known for framing scribbles and first drafts from its patrons, in some sad attempt to cling to any fame (or infamy) that might brush past it. One such draft was a love poem that Ophelia Jeffington-Faircroft had written for her secret lover, a girl called Mabel Loucroft-Smyth. However, Ophelia had been proposed to by Sir Something-of-Whatever from the city of I've-Stopped-Listening, and poor Mabel had threatened exposure when she had been

103

dumped. Or, rather, steadfastly ignored in the hopes that she'd go away. And her plot – and Ophelia's chance at happiness with a boring but comfortable house, and a boring but comfortable husband – hinged on this poem hanging in the Eshneal.

'Mabel has always been of a jealous disposition, that minx! She cannot be allowed to get away with this!' Ophelia had screeched. After that, the Rat Prince had given up on demanding and begging for discretion and had simply left the back street where they met, directions and objectives in hand.

The windowpanes on the Eshneal were old, the wood softened and the paint flaking. The lock on the inside of the window was older than Ida herself; she knew they didn't make them anymore, that was for certain. Once the street died down for the night, and the   constables were safely far away on their stroll (their meandering could barely be called a beat), it was all too easy to slither down the side of the building, press her slight weight against the panels, and jiggle the   window pane up and down, up and down, until…

Click. Ida pushed the windowpane open, slipped through the smallest gap she could manage, and dropped down to the floor, as silent as a cat. Or a rat. Back when she first heard the nickname she was given by the citizens of Loxport, Ida had privately seethed that it couldn't be something classier, more fitting of her skills, and less grimy. But, over time, she had grown to love The Rat Prince, even leaning into his darker image;

learning how to tilt her head so that the glare from the streetlamps caught on her goggles just so, lowering her voice even further to a gravelly whisper. It became another layer of disguise, and it was fun.

The main room of the Eshneal smelled like lavender, stale smoke and overconfidence. The tables and chairs were endearingly tatty, and, just as Mabel had said, the walls were covered with paper. Some sheets were fresh and gleaming white, some yellow and curled at the edges. And there, at the top of the stairwell, was The Rat Prince's prize for the evening.

Even to gutter trash like Ida, the penmanship was sloppy. This was rushed, passionate, from-the-dark-reaches-of-my-soul stuff. And still Ophelia had rhymed 'Mabel' with not only 'able', but 'a bell.' Miss Loucroft-Smyth was definitely coming away from this tryst better off. Ida peeled it gently from the wall,   taking care to leave no trace of sticking-gum behind. There would be a conspicuous gap on the Eshneal building wall; Ida didn't have time to rearrange the entire display. But by the time anyone discovered this particular piece was missing, it would be sodden ashes floating out to sea on the Lox, and who would be able to remember the exact specifications of adoration it contained? Besides, its spot would soon be claimed by another budding wordsmith.

Ida rolled the paper up into a tight scroll and slotted into a hidden pocket in her trousers. As she turned back towards the window to make her escape, she heard the brash voices of two constables about halfway down the road. They must have been harassing some poor flower girl out after dark, possibly sneaking home from some tryst before Mam and Dad realised she was gone.

'So where you off to, love? Need an escort, ha ha.'

'Ha… no, no thank you…'

'What, not a fan of a man in uniform?'

From the safety of the shadows, Ida rolled her eyes. Those flower girls put up with a lot. So much of their job was about selling little songs and giggles as much as posies. Ida didn't have a lot of dignity in the daylight hours, but at least she didn't have to smile and simper for her supper. At least, as long as Casterbury stayed a bachelor.

They were herding the flower girl up the street, towards the fancier, well-lit part of Loxport. Towards the Eshneal. Which was fine for the flower girl, less so for The Rat Prince and his open window. Ida had to make them turn around.

There was a back door that led into the alleyway behind the Eshneal. Mercifully, it was only locked by means of two sliding bolts, so Ida had it open in the blink of an eye. Now, something to cause a distraction.

Two dustbins, overflowing with glass bottles, stood illuminated by a far-off lamp. Perfect. Ida reared back and kicked the first bin with all her strength, sending both bins and their contents clattering down the alleyway.

'Watch where ya goin', ya tit – I'll 'ave ye!' Ida roared in her deepest, fullest, most comical Loxportian accent, then closed the back doors quickly and silently as she heard two pairs of footsteps and shouts of 'Halt! Loxport constabulary!' By the time the constables were at the back door, Ida had sped back through the Eshneal's front room, dove through the gap in the window, and was in the process of digging her fingers into the wooden pane to close it when –

'Thank you, for that.'

The Rat Prince whirled to see the flower girl standing on the opposite side of the cobbled street, twisting her bonnet in her hands. He straightened.

'You didn't see anything, yeah?' he said, advancing on the girl in a way that would have made Reggie Powell flinch. But this girl, with her blonde ringlets and her daisy-print dress, didn't budge.

'Was just saying thank you; no need to get snippy.'

'Well...' The Rat Prince adjusted his goggles. 'Keep it that way.'

The flower girl tossed her ringlets and smiled. 'You could have just ran out the back, you know. But you didn't.'

'It's fun to mess with them,' The Rat Prince countered, hopping up onto the window ledge. 'I'd prefer if you didn't see which way I go.'

'Fair enough.'

The Rat Prince waited until the girl turned the corner, the daisies on her dress turning baby blue in the bioluminescent light, and then scaled the building, swung up onto the flat stone roof, and took off at a run. Ida leapt over buildings at random, enjoying the fresh breeze on her face. The city had been warm of late, and the salt-dusted wind felt nice.

You're going soft, Ida Finn. First Edith, then Clem, and now saving random girls from the clutches of constables…

It was a happy accident. Obviously.

'I told those constables,' a voice drifted up from the streets below, tingled with laughter, 'that I didn't need an escort.'

The Rat Prince skidded to a halt halfway along a row of terraced houses. Down below, the flower girl leaned against the low brick wall of a garden, house key in hand. She lifted one hand in a wave.

'Goodnight, Mister Rat Prince.'

The shadowy figure on her rooftop glided away without another word. One could almost say he was embarrassed.

Chapter Nineteen

———

Clink.

'Ida.'

Clunk.

'Ida!' A crack as the last stone hit the windowpane a little harder than expected. Ida opened her window and looked down three stories at the mane of red hair standing in her back yard.

'I-daah,' Edith sang, 'come out to plaa-ay.'

Ida wordlessly disappeared back into the depths of her room. The note from Edith saying she'd be paying a visit sat forgotten on her dressing table. She'd been so looking forward to doing nothing. She'd woken up especially early so she could do double-duty on her stretches in anticipation for doing nothing. And she still had to go down to Tarnish Street before she could.

'I-daah,' the voice sang again through her window, 'I've got you a pre-seent...'

Ida glanced out her window again. Edith was rattling a bag of sugared almonds as large as her head, grinning like a lunatic.

What the hell. Tarnish Street can wait for once. It didn't take much to persuade Ida not to go. It wasn't like it was the most fun part of her day at the best of times.

Ida slipped on her purple dress, left a scribbled note for Lucinda – just in case she thought her maid been abducted – and closed the kitchen door behind her. Edith wrapped her up in a huge, shoulder blade   popping hug. It was like being enveloped in a feather duvet with a python inside.

Oh. Alright, then.

Ida patted Edith gently on the shoulder.

'Hello.'

'Hi!' Edith chirped, handing over the bag of almonds. 'You didn't reply to my letter, so I thought I'd bring some bribery to get you outside!'

'Always a good idea. So,' Ida said, in between crunches, 'what grand adventure have you planned for us today?'

'A riverboat ride!'

Ida cocked her head to one side. Edith was almost hopping from foot to foot.

'Really?'

'Really! I heard one of the gents at the Acutus talking about it. They're renting boats on the river in Calista Gardens. You can take them out for the whole day, and they have motors, so you can probably see the entire city in no time. It's only ten Athenas, so we could go halves, and still get a cake from the Boathouse after. Or maybe the fancy park has an even fancier tearoom!'

'Or,' Ida suggested, 'we could get two cakes at the Boathouse and save ourselves the sea-sickness.'

'Oh, don't be such a misery guts,' Edith said, poking

her friend between the ribs. 'It'll be a laugh.'

The two girls strolled away from the bustling streets and into the quiet, green space of the park. Most of their conversation revolved around their employers; or, rather, complaining about them.

'...So then, he says '"Lucinda, you look absolutely breath-taking. A mermaid, a siren, a rare ocean jewel!"'

'And she fell for it?'

'Like a ton of bricks.'

Edith giggled, fluttering her eyelashes and swooning against Ida.

'Oh, Devon, Devon! Hold me in your arms! Let me stroke your moustache, it's so... manly!'

Ida's laugh was a soft bark at the back of her throat, pretending to struggle under her friend's weight.

'Get off me, you idiot.'

Edith swatted her arm.

'Not a speck of romance in your entire body, Ida, I swear it.'

'And you're such a master of the heart, are you?' Ida laughed. 'Have you even spoken to your Scientist woman yet?'

Edith's face fell instantly. She ran her hand through her hair, fingers snagging on a few tangles the breeze had blown into her curls. She actually looked really upset. Ida had thought this thing with Doctor Malko was all in good fun, like everything else with Edith. She reached out and brushed the back of Edith's hand with her fingertips. Her skin was warm and soft and slightly dry over the knuckles.

'Oh Lord, Edie; I didn't mean it like that…'

Edie? Where did that come from?

'No, I know you were just teasing,' Edith said, knocking her own hand against Ida's affectionately. 'I shouldn't be such a wet blanket. It's just – I feel so stupid, you know?'

Ida didn't know. Not really. 'Oh yeah, Edith, I know all about love. I found myself quite flustered just yesterday when a boy was sweating at a forge near me. A sweaty, dirty, probably smelly boy made the butterflies in my stomach do a tap dance up into my chest. And I don't know why! Did I also mention that I'm a famous burglar and I stole something from him only a few days hence? How embarrassing!'

Calista Gardens was a very different animal to Big Pond Park. Perfectly manicured lawns lined by perfectly pedigreed plants, with a river cutting through it as clean and cool-looking as a bolt of blue-grey silk. There was no sound, apart from the polite chirpings of a blackbird. Ida had a sudden urge to swing from the trees and hoot, just to see what would happen. As they finally reached the river, Edith's step quickened. There were boats lined up against the shoreline, each one tied to a post hammered into the soft bank of the river. The tiny replicas of schooners, white sails gleaming against the eggshell-blue sky, bobbed while their owner paced back and forth, calling out prices and promises to see the most prestigious sights of the city. Edith looked at the immaculate price board next to him and made a small noise of disappointment in her throat.

'Oh, bugger; it's ten Athenas for just a twenty-minute ride! Each! I must have heard wrong at the Acutus.'

'I can pay, if you like…' Ida said, digging in her pockets for her purse. She had cash to spare, after all. Edith shook her head.

'I can't ask you to pay that, Ida. That's extortionate for two maids to pay.'

She shrugged, pretending not to be disappointed.

'Never mind, Ida; let's walk back up to Big Pond Park and –'

Ida paused, for just a second, to think. Then, she got Edith's attention with a squeeze of the wrist, pulling her down so that her ear was level with Ida's mouth.

'Keep the boatsman distracted. I've got an idea.'

'What?'

'Just, you know, talk to him about prices, or something. Haggle. I'll signal for you.'

Edith waited for an explanation. None came. Ida just motioned her forward. So, she sidled up to the man kneeling on the grass, tying and retying his knots. Of course, he was the only person in Loxport not instantly charmed by Edith's dimpled smile and ample curves, and just gave her a curt nod as she approached.

'Um. Hello.'

'G'mornin', miss.'

'It's a nice day, isn't it?'

'Lovely day for a ride up the Lox, miss. Ten Athenas for a trip around the river, be back by teatime?'

'How about five Athenas?'

'That gets you some spun sugar around the corner, miss. Nothing on my boats, I'm afraid.'

'What about, um, five Athenas and a Hermes?'

The boatsman straightened to look at Edith. Behind him, Ida wandered away, hands in the pockets of her dress, staring into the middle distance, out over the queue of tied-up boats, as cool as you please. To an unknowing observer, she was just a passer-by, enjoying the view. Now, which knots looked the loosest...

'Miss. I can't haggle on my prices.'

'But...you see...'

That one.

The boatsman moved to turn away from Edith just as Ida knelt and began untying a boat's moorings, her fingers moving in a blur. Edith must have seen her and put two and two together, because lunged for the boatsman's hand, kneeling in supplication before him. Ida watched her desperately try to force tears into her eyes.

'But... but it's my birthday!'

Edith had already told Ida her birthday was in November. She was a terrible liar. The boatsman gave Edith a long, stern look.

'Look, pet. I've got things to do. You can't afford it, so go find something else to entertain yourself with before I flag down a constable to move you along.' Then Ida was by her side, hauling her up by the arm.

'Edith, get up. It's not that important. Sorry, sir, my friend can be quite dramatic, sometimes.'

Relief flashed across the boatsman's face and he

nodded curtly before turning back to his work. Ida spun Edith around, seemingly leading her away, along the line of schooners.

'Furthest boat along. When I say, go.'

The words came sliding out of Ida's almost-closed mouth. Edith laughed, nervously.

'Very funny, Ida. Let's just forget –'

'Now.'

Ida's hands shoved hard at Edith's back, propelling her forward, towards the boat. She had no choice but to run, both feet pounding in the loam of the riverbank, before lifting off the ground, willed by Ida's shout of 'jump!' She landed on her hands and knees against damp wood with a thud. Ida hauled the boat away from the shore with a startling amount of strength, leaping nimbly over the washboard, yanking on the cord connected to the rudder as she landed. The boat surged forward, waves of cold river water splashing over Edith's back, making her shriek. They were away from the dock before the boatsman could catch them. They could hear his bellowed curses even as they rounded a corner and he disappeared from sight.

Suddenly, the world seemed very quiet. Edith reached over and grabbed Ida's arm.

'Ida! What on earth..?'

Ida whirled on her. Edith fell backwards in the boat, eyes wide.

'Ida? What's going on?'

Ida couldn't move, suddenly. Her breath was hitching

hard and painful in her chest. The euphoria of the heist and the getaway gone as suddenly as it had arrived when she had taken Edith's wrist in her hand and decided what she was going to do. That she was going to cross the paths of her two lives, to do something risky and stupid and pointless and not even worth any money; to make her friend happy.

Ida's face cracked open in a guilty smile.

'We'll take it back... eventually.'

A long, silent beat. And then the two were collapsed against the boat's rail, spluttering with scandalised, triumphant laughter.

Chapter Twenty

———

For a while, they powered the motor, propelling themselves away from any chance of being spotted by the boatsman, or any constable he happened to collar. The scenery changed from trees and strolling couples to townhouses and museums. They'd left the confines of the park and were travelling through Loxport itself. They passed under the Loxport Bridge, and chatted idly about whether the upcoming bio-luminescence was a good idea; Edith was for, Ida was against, for reasons of jellyfish. Carriages rattled by, either strapped to a team of horses or with new engines puffing out grey clouds, while crowds of young scholars moved between buildings like shoals of chatty fish. Reluctant to get tangled up in the industrial area of the city beyond – the mouth of the river was teeming with ports and docks and huge cargo ships – Ida killed the engine, letting them drift aimlessly along at a snail's pace. Edith let her fingers trail by the side of the boat, watching her reflection distort on the water's surface as she talked, her skirts spread out over the seat so they'd dry a little.

'...then Kate had a ladder in her stockings, and she refused to leave the house until I found her some new ones. Why on earth she didn't tell me the night before, I will never understand; she never really wants to talk to me anymore…'

'She's twelve. It's normal. I was a moody little brat at twelve.'

'…so once that was sorted, I had to run all the way to the Acutus to make it on time, so I was out of breath, and my hair came loose from the pins –'

'Shock, horror. Alert the constables.'

'Shut up,' Edith flicked water at Ida's face. 'So, I got there barely on time, at my wit's end, and what was my first order?'

'Let me guess – a green tea and a shortbread?'

Ida had, somewhat unwillingly, memorised every detail about a woman she'd seen in person a handful of times.

'Of course it was! And there I am, looking like a… like a bedraggled beetroot. I couldn't even speak, I just plonked her order down in front of her and ran into the back. I didn't even take the tray.'

Ida lounged on the other side of the deck, squinting in the sunshine.

'Do you ever speak to her?'

'… sometimes.'

'What was the last thing you said to her?'

Edith shifted in her seat.

'Cook changed the recipe of the shortbread. They use vanilla in the dough, now. She said it was an improvement. I told her I'd pass the message on.'

'And you say I'm not a romantic.'

'Oh, come off it, Ida. It's one thing to pretend, but I'm

never actually going to talk to her, not properly. She's a famous scientist. She's been all over the world, she's got a wing in a museum named after her. I just serve tea.'

'That's not all you do.'

'No?' 'You have a double life. Edith Webb: Boat Thief. Feared and adored around the globe.'

'You're so funny.'

'I know.'

Ida shuffled over to sit at Edith's side.

'Seriously, though. Don't let other people tell you who you are. Or what you are and are not good enough for. A friend of mine was just talking to me about that. Not letting them take away part of… what is it?'

Edith was looking at her, a sly expression slinking onto her face.

'A friend, hm? I thought I was the only one that had found a crack in Ida Finn's armor.'

Ida would not blush. She fought to keep her face neutral at all costs. She would not think about sweat on the back of necks or rolled up sleeves. Or warm palms. Edith leaned forward, her hands clutching at each other in front of her lips, which were pressed tightly together as she fought back a wild laugh.

'Edith?'

'Are they a lady or a gent?'

'Edith!'

'Well I don't know! You've never talked about romantic encounters…'

Romantic encounters?! Was that what that was back

at the smithy? Clem should have notified her if it was, that was very inconsiderate of him.

'And I'm still not talking about them. Clem is just someone that I met –'

'Oooh, Clem!'

'Shut up!'

The boat rocked dangerously as Ida shoved Edith, who fell over dramatically cackling.

'Tell me everything!'

'There's nothing to tell,' Ida said. 'I think we should find a place to dock the boat and get back home.'

'Not until you tell me about this Clem,' Edith demanded, righting herself. 'I told you all about the Scientist, I think the least you can do is –'

'I don't know, alright?!'

That came out sharper than Ida had intended. Edith's smile dropped away. Ida did blush then. She slid off the seat and onto the curved, warm floor of the boat.

'Sorry, Edie. I've just never had to worry about this before. I don't know what he is; is he a friend, or is he just someone I don't hate? There's only ever been one box in my mind: people I work for. And then I had a new box for you. And then Lucinda doesn't quite fit in the first box anymore, and then Clem doesn't fit in any box and it's hard to think when you haven't been sleeping and I'm so tired all the time and I keep dreaming about my mam...'

She was almost talking to herself, now: staring down at the panels of light brown wood beneath her. That was the most she'd talked about herself in years. Edith scooted towards Ida, and took her hand.

'Well,' she said, 'the good thing is, you don't have to decide right now, do you? And if you ever do want to talk about him, you know where I am. We'll steal another boat and talk about our feelings.'

They were drifting now through the residential streets of Loxport. Streets full of flower girls and dock-workers, kids pushing their baby siblings in old perambulators, shops with tatty signs selling the most delicious bread or pies or macaroons you would find in Loxport, if only you knew where to look. And, somewhere beyond all that, was Tarnish Street. Ida hadn't quite realised where they were, and her chest twisted slightly.

Between the two of them, Ida and Edith steered the boat into a grassy bank of the river Lox, where it connected with the earth with a bump that threw both girls off balance. They carefully clambered ashore, and Ida shoved the boat back into the Lox, where it caught the current again. Edith saluted.

'Godspeed, little boat. I hope the owner finds it,' she said.

'If not, someone at the docks could make an earning off the lumber.'

'Ida!' Edith laughed.

'Sorry.'

'Look, I should go. We're almost at my house, actually. I've had a really good day, even including the theft.'

She waved over her shoulder, turned onto a cobbled

terrace, and was gone from sight. Ida watched for a long while as the boat found its way into the current. It snagged on something; a tiny whirlpool, a stick, maybe even a piece of junk submerged below the water. Then, after a moment or two of futility, whatever had a hold on the boat was gone, and the little vessel flowed behind some trees, and out of sight. Ida shoved her hands in the pockets of her dress and turned towards Tarnish Street.

Chapter Twenty-One

———

Might as well get it out of the way while I'm here, Ida thought. No point in going all the way back to Juniper Avenue to come back. It made sense. It was efficient. So why did Ida's feet feel like they were made of lead?

As she walked along the uneven cobblestone back alleys and took the same turns she'd taken all her life, a few people nodded to her or raised their hand in a casual wave. In this part of town, everyone knew everyone; your mam had babysat the neighbour's kids when they were small, and now you were as good as family. This was the same in the criminal community; someone's sister was always stepping out with someone worth knowing, or who had done you a solid back in the day. And the two communities overlapped, of course. Ida wasn't worried about someone putting two and two together when she was on a job, though. Molly Finn's daughter wasn't from around here anymore. She was working as a maid in one of those fancy houses no one went near. She got out.

Number Forty-One Tarnish Street looked very similar to the houses around it; part of a slightly shabby, tightly packed together terrace, with gutters that could use a clean and a yard door that flaked paint like snow when Ida opened it.

The kitchen counters were the way Ida had always remembered them: bare. Oh, they never starved, but there was never anything beyond a simple breakfast of apples from the market, and bread and cold meat in the evening. Lucinda would have a fit if she were deprived of her cakes and creams in this manner. Ida's sugared almond addiction had started right in this room, in fact. She had smuggled her prize past her family so she could scoff the lot in the peace of her and her mam's shared bedroom.

A woman sat in a rocking chair beside the fire, knitting. Every time she came, Ida thought her grandmother looked smaller. She wore a thick woollen shawl over her shoulders, and the way she hunched over her knitting needles made her look like the leaves of a fern, curling in on herself. Ida knelt beside the rocking chair, her insides already feeling like they were lined with lead.

'Hello, Nan.'

'Ah, Ida love,' her grandmother said, accepting the kiss Ida quickly placed on her dry, soft cheek. 'I feel like I haven't seen you in a long while!'

'Last Wednesday, Nan. I always come over on a Wednesday.'

'Well,' Ida's grandmother said, setting the rocking chair swaying as she continued with her knitting, 'I've been feeling so poorly recently, and time goes by so slowly when you're old, you know?'

'What's happened?' Ida asked, suddenly concerned. 'Is it your knees again? Do you want me to send for a nurse? I can organise one to be here next week, so I'm here too –'

'Oh, don't bother, Ida. That lovely boy from down the road, Thomas, you know who I mean?'

'No, Nan.'

'You do. Thomas!'

Ida had no idea who Thomas was. She assumed he'd held her for ten minutes when she was two. It didn't matter. 'What does Thomas do for you, Nan?'

'Well,' the older woman said, her needles clacking as she spoke, 'he goes to the shop for me, and gets me a bottle of Coriander oil, and I take that when I get a pain.'

'Nan, Coriander oil won't do anything for joint pain.'

'He's such a nice boy, Thomas.'

'Nan…'

'He says, 'Lizzie, you just tell us what we can do, we know you're on your own now and have no one to turn to for help since your Ida left…"

Ida's pride was seething already. Less than five minutes in; that might be a new record.

'Nan,' she said, trying to keep her voice level, 'if you want anything, I'd really rather you asked me than people down the street.'

'Well, I don't want to bother you, what with your busy life, up in that fancy mansion you call home now.'

'It's my employer's house, Nan. It's not my home.'

'Did you ever talk to her about adopting you, like I said? Thomas' wife Doreen said she heard of something like that, where a posh woman took in a poor orphan child because she couldn't have any herself. She didn't have the bits, the doctor told her…'

This was not the first time this topic of conversation had come up. And no, Ida had not asked Lucinda Belmonte to adopt her.

'Nan,' she explained, for the tenth time, 'I'm nineteen. I'm an adult, now.'

'You're still a child. You don't know anything. But I'm just glad you have a decent, stable job, Ida love,' her grandmother said, setting her knitting down and staring into the fire. 'Unlike your mother. Feckless, she was. I do wish you were a little closer to home, though. Why not ask Joseph Mann if he has any jobs going at the bakery, then you could move back home?'

Ida's mam had tried to learn to bake bread herself. It ended up with her and Ida grinding flour into each other's hair and laughing so hard that Nan separated them. It wasn't one of Molly Finn's talents, baking. Instead, she would come home most nights with what she'd call her 'bag of tricks' – various shiny things she'd lifted from drunks as they staggered out of the opium dens and the gentlemen's clubs. Watches, tie pins, money clips straining against wads of ten-Athena notes. She'd dump them all on the floor, and would teach Ida what was good to sell and what was pretty but useless. Nan would sniff, snatch up something that interested her and make herself scarce. Mam would push her goggles up onto the top of her head, and grin wildly at Ida.

'Where you're going, Ida hinny,' she said, cupping her under the chin. 'This will be everywhere. This, and more. You'll be tripping over beautiful jewels, and famous art pieces, and blueprints for gadgets you can't even imagine. We just need to get you there.'

Ida's mother had been a falcon. She stalked Loxport's rich, swooped in, took what she needed, and was gone. She wanted more for Ida than that. She wanted Ida to become a cuckoo.

Ida got her first job as a live-in maid when she was twelve. He was an old man, with a wide range of elite contacts and a mild terror of the young people that worked for him. Her mother was thrilled. She wanted to know everything. Not just about the trinkets, but what her life was like now; how she was eating, what the house she worked in smelled like, what her employer wore, what breed of dog he owned…

They were planning her first big heist when she died. Consumption, according to the doctor when he finally visited. It hit her so quickly that she died the next morning, Ida's hand clutching hers as if it would do something to stop her leaving. After Ida had completed the job, she sat on a rooftop with the pearls she'd stolen shoved in her pocket, knotted around each other, and cried until her throat screamed and her vision was too blurry for her to make it home. She'd blamed her lateness for work the next morning on 'girl sickness' and her employer had let her off with a fearful look and double-dusting-duty.

The Rat Prince had only had a name for three years, but he had been around much, much longer.

'…all those crimes she committed,' Ida's nan continued,

'and with a little baby and a mother at home, waiting for her! Selfish. I'm surprised she got to die in her own bed, and not in prison. Should have settled down, found you a father figure instead of tarring you with the same delinquent brush. She wasn't the prettiest girl in Loxport, but she could have found someone. You look like her, too, both skinny little things, like struck matches with that short hair, the pair of you. I hear about your antics, you know,' she continued, barely wasting a breath. '"Rat Prince" this, "Rat Prince" that. What a waste of potential. But I suppose you never had a chance, with my Molly for your mother.'

Ida's mam's face swam in front of her vision. Molly could laugh this stuff off: roll her eyes at Nan's barbs and go about her day, unbothered. Untouched. Happy, despite it all. Ida couldn't. Ida was nothing like her mam.

'…lucky I don't tell anyone what I know, isn't it? I could, you know. Thomas and Doreen are always asking after you. But I'd never dob my family in like that.'

Her voice sounded so much like Ida's mam's. The same musical Loxportian accent, the same emphasis on the same words. But the words were so different, like she was a dark reflection of the woman Ida had lost. But Nan was all she had left to tie her back to her roots. Back to her mam. Her mam would want this. She would.

'Well, Ida,' her grandmother said, tossing her knitting into her lap in a gesture of finality, 'it's been lovely to see you, but I suppose you must be off, back to your lovely posh house. Just pop the money on the side, there's a good lass.'

And here it was. The moment Ida's been dreading since she decided to come to Tarnish Street instead of heading home. She hadn't brought her Nan's share of the profits.

'Er…well, Nan. I haven't got the money with me. It's at home, in my wardrobe, but, see, I went out with a friend this morning…'

'Oh?' Ida's grandmother tilted her head, bird-like, as if Ida were suddenly speaking gibberish. 'You decided not to bring me any money?'

'No, Nan, it's not that.'

'Well, I just don't know what I'll do, then…'

Her voice was wavering. Ida's gaze plummeted to the floor.

'I was just in the area,' she mumbled, 'and I thought I'd pop in now and see you, rather than…rather than…'

Nan wasn't listening. She'd turned back to the fire, looking into the flames with a look of wretched despondency. Ida felt like a child again. Guilt washed over her like a wave of tar, cold and heavy and black.

'Nan… I'll bring it this week and next when I come back. I promise. And you've got enough to get by, haven't you? You've got food?'

'I suppose,' her grandmother sniffed, 'I will manage, somehow. Rely on the kindness of neighbors. I'm just surprised, love, I didn't even think you had friends. Never did when you were little, that's for sure.'

Ida flinched. After all this time, she still flinched from her grandmother's words. And that, the embarrassment of still allowing it to hurt, made it all the more painful.

Apart from the sound of the flames crackling and the creak of the chair as it rocked back and forth, the room was heavy with silence. Ida felt like she was drowning in it. She wandered into the living room, buying time for conversation to start up again. The rug in the middle of the room was the same one she knew from childhood, just more worn out and scratchy. The air was warm and thick from the fire that burned in the grate, which made Ida's skin prickle. Across the mantelpiece were a few odds and ends: a romance pamphlet that had been popular a month or so ago, a vase of flowers just about to wilt. And two coffee cans filled with dull yellow Athenas, with a few Hermes sprinkled throughout like chips of ice.

Ida turned back to say something, say anything. But she knew when she had been dismissed. She'd danced this dance for years. So instead, she said her goodbyes.

'See you next week, Nan.'

'Oh, you're going, Ida?'

'I need to get back to the house, in case I'm needed. See you soon. Love you, Nan.'

'G'bye, dear. You'll remember next week, yes?

'… yes.'

'Good lass.'

Ida left the house, breathed the fresh air deep into her lungs, and resisted the temptation to slam the yard door behind her over and over again until it was nothing but splinters.

About an hour later, Clem opened the door of his

smithy for some fresh air, and found a note wedged into the doorjamb.

I'll do it.
RP.

Chapter Twenty-Two

––––––

The rain spat onto the smooth pavement of Innovation Court as a dark shape slashed its way over the Loxport skyline.

Ida's mind was a storm. Anger and guilt, confusion and indignation swirled together, blending and separating and mixing again in new combinations. Somewhere deep inside her brain, a tiny part of her mind was slamming a hammer against her skull and screaming *this is why you don't get attached to people* over and over again. *Because you're not worth it. You can't even have a normal day out with a friend, let alone support your own family. You're a useless, angry, pathetic criminal, and the only person who knew you – really, truly knew you and loved you anyway – is dead.* She'd run all the way home from Tarnish Street and spent the remainder of the day pacing the floor of her room like a restless, caged animal. As soon as the sun disappeared behind the rooftops, she'd thrown on her Rat Prince garb. She needed this. She needed to feel the pounding of her feet on shale rooftops, the sensation of hurling herself from ledge to ledge. If she ran fast enough, she could leave Lucinda's pity, Nan's disgust, Edith's confusion and Casterbury's sneers behind her. Maybe then they'd blow out onto the North Sea on some errant night breeze and leave her alone.

She landed on the rooftop of Devon Casterbury's neighbour and slunk across the tiles. All the lights on the ground floor of the three-floor home were blazing, and shadows were thrown out across the immaculate lawn as people moved from room to room. Devon was obviously having some kind of social event. That didn't matter. She was doing this job tonight, come hell or high water. This was what she was good at. The only thing she was good at.

There was a window open on the third floor. She dropped into the back garden and clambered up the drainpipe onto a window ledge. The window opened outwards from the top, and there was barely enough room, but thankfully Ida was a skinny little thing. Like a struck match. She was in a bedroom; an unused one, from the neatly pressed linens and the subtle smell of stale lavender soap on the bedsheets. Casterbury's house was large enough to comfortably house a family of five or more and, like Lucinda, he could only ever use a fraction of it day-to-day. Meanwhile Ida and her mother had slept in the same bedroom until she was seven, often curled up together in the same bed.

Never mind that. Orientate yourself, Ida: where is he, and where would he hide the gem? Ida crept to the bedroom doorway and flattened herself against the wall. Raucous laughter drifted up to her from downstairs, along with the clink of glasses.

'Trust Casterbury to have such damned good luck!' one voice boomed, to a great chorus of guffaws. 'You never did say how you obtained the thing, Devon?' said another voice, slurring slightly. 'Do ssspill your sseeecrets…'

'Unlike the wine you christened my carpet with, Parker, I shall keep my secrets safely contained.' Casterbury's voice bulldozed the rest into submission. None were so loud, so confident, so utterly, repulsively posh. 'The matter for true discussion is what it can do. I think this little gem could revolutionise the technological standing of Loxport. For the right investors, that is.'

The curving half-moon shape of the hallway was dark; the dining quarters below looked like a lake made of light. Ida turned her goggles off and crept out, silently, to get a better look. The carpet was soft and lush underneath the palms of her hands as she crouched, nose almost to the floor, and peeked down. Casterbury was standing in the middle of a group of men, all wearing suits. Some had medals pinned to their lapels, some had elegant cravats or pocket-watches. All moneyed men, of one strand or another. Waitresses in Acutus Club uniforms milled around from guest to guest, serving pastel-coloured drinks and savoury nibbles.

Casterbury produced the green gem with an ill-advised flourish. It dawned on Ida that he'd had a waistcoat and pocket-square tailored in matching shades of green, and she'd never longed to spit from a vantage point so badly.

'This, my friends,' he announced, 'is Kaelinite. The Lightning Stone. Barely ever seen outside of myth, apart from by so-called explorers more interested in fantasy than science –'

'Odessa Malko!' Parker roared from the back of the crowd. It sounded like someone slapped him across the back of the head for his remark, but Casterbury laughed genially.

'We digress, gents. Most accounts of Kaelinite have been circumstantial, and it has never made its way into the civilized world... before tonight. I have it from an exceptionally reliable and very expensive source that this is a record-setting amount. This, my friends –'

Here, Casterbury waved the gem back and forth forcefully enough to generate a slow, burning light, but not rashly enough to cause a glowing beacon like Ida had on the roof of the Schuyler.

'— this gem, and its ability to harness kinetic energy, could catapult Loxport – and its greatest minds – to unprecedented levels of advancement. Now,' he said, stepping into the crowd and away from Ida's vision, 'why don't we have our own little exhibition here tonight, gents? Tell me what this gem inspires in you – and the profits attached, of course!'

Another great roar of laughter, and a bubbling of voices all shouting to be heard. Ida leaned her head silently against the gleaming wooden banister and winced.

He had the gem in his horrible, sweaty palm. He wouldn't be letting it go any time soon, now when he was holding court like this. Well, information can be valuable too, she thought, glancing around in the dark to make sure she was still alone. Perhaps she would hear something useful tonight.

I'll get something out of this job. I swear it.

She caught twenty snippets of twenty different conversations, all happening at once.

'From here to London in a matter of hours, Casterbury! Imagine how envious the good old 'Southern Powerhouse' will be when they see our dirigibles flying overhead at that speed...'

'...projections of moving art, right in the home! Imagine your next dinner party in the middle of Isle of La Grande Jatte...'

A tall, bespectacled man pushed his way through the chatter and stooped to speak in Casterbury's ear. Ida couldn't hear what he said, but his brows were knitted tightly together, and he fiddled anxiously with his cufflinks. Before long, Casterbury shoved the man away with a veneer of playfulness that was paper-thin.

'Oh, do come off it, Bridgers – curses?! I thought you were a historian, man.'

The gent – Bridgers – stood up straighter, attempting to come off as authoritative.

'Devon, I am a historian. And if you know the nickname for Kaelinite, you should also know that name has a duel meaning. "After the Lightning bares its teeth..."'

'"The darkness swallows you whole," I know,' Casterbury finished, wafting his hand in Bridgers' face like he was a bad smell. 'I read all about it. Bridgers, it's a fairy story. Meant to ward off thieves, brigands, that sort of thing. Now, go have a drink, find a nice waitress to flirt with, and leave me alone, there's a good chap.'

'Devon, I'm married. To your cousin…'

'Casterbury, may we speak?'

A tall man in a dark, pressed uniform stepped out of the crowd, as if the throngs of men around him were no more consequential than mist. Ida felt her heart constrict. A constable. A high-up constable, with an immaculate uniform, a pristinely groomed moustache and a gleaming Detective's badge.

'All this talk of art and industry is very grand, very fitting for a place like Loxport,' the man said, leading Casterbury away from the noise and pouring him a drink. 'But so many minds of art and industry living in one city are the very reason we need to be focusing more on… ahem, protection.'

'I absolutely agree, Detective Oakden,' Casterbury was saying, handing his suddenly empty glass to a passing maid. 'I've had a few run-ins with the criminal type myself, of late.'

That treacherous, self-serving…

'Oh? Is that part of why you look so tired tonight, Casterbury? Not sleeping?'

'Oh, no, my lad – I haven't been sleeping, it's true. Plagued by nightmares, utterly plagued. But I put it down to a simple bout of food poisoning. Can't teach those cooks at the Acutus a thing, what?'

'Quite. I wouldn't know. But that's beside the point. My career – the careers of all Loxport constables – have been marred by repeated attacks from The Rat Prince, and all the other reprobates of the lower sect of the city. There isn't a household in Loxport that would not benefit from some form of protection – for their blueprints, for their inventions, for their families – from people like him.'

This Detective Oakden's face was hard and blank as he stared into the middle distance, clearly imagining a noose around a certain neck. Casterbury's own gaze was distant, but a smile bloomed under his moustache.

'I think, Detective Oakden, that is a capital idea. And an idea that could make us a lot of capital, what?'

'I'm sure.'

And so this was the Detective Oakden Ida had heard so much about. The stern, rule-loving constable that had sent Daniel running home with his tail between his legs, who was now moments away from securing a powerful new energy source specifically to hunt Ida down.

Clarity hit Ida like a wave of ice water. She needed to leave. Now.

'Hello? Who's there?'

A voice from the stairwell up to the third floor made Ida – still crouched on the floor, almost leaning over the pillars of the banister to listen – whirl. She could make out the form of a girl, a maid's cloth cap atop her head, coming up the stairs. She paused. An achingly long   second of stillness. Ida moved to stand. The maid opened her mouth to scream. Ida ran.

In the darkness of the unused bedroom, she ploughed straight into the dressing table, the edge connecting hard with her bony hip. Ida bit back a yelp and spun. She could hear footsteps thundering up the stairs to the maid's aid – that constable among them, more likely than not. Ida wrenched the window open as far as it would go, the wood cracking under her as she scrambled through the gap. The light in the bedroom flared into life just as she connected with the lawn with a heavy thud. Instantly she was up and running, climbing buildings and leaping from them blindly. Her vision was blurred and tilting, her heart ready to burst from her chest and run all the way back to Tarnish Street. Where she belonged.

And then her legs skidded out from underneath her, the world tipped itself upside down, and she ended up sprawled across the stones of Sixsmith Street, in a heap in a filthy alleyway, breath scorching in her chest, legs weak from running. And that's where Clem found her.

Chapter Twenty-Three

———

'Ida? Oh, god! Ida, come on, stand up.'

How did he know who she was? No one had ever recognised her. Ida raised her head up from its cradle on her knees to see a familiar shock of ginger hair hovering above her.

Hang on…

'My goggles,' she cried, jumping to her feet and looking around her wildly. 'Where are my goggles?' I can't have lost her goggles. I can't have.

'Ida…' No, no no no no –

'Ida! They're here, just stop or you're going to stand on them.'

Clem whisked the goggles from under Ida's feet, holding them in front of her by the straps. She must have knocked them off her face when she fell. Relief and shame coursed through Ida's body, hot as acid. She snatched them back, shoving them over her eyes.

'What is going on?' Clem asked.

'Get out of my way,' Ida snarled, her voice cracking as she pushed Clem aside and stormed off, towards the entrance to the alley. Storming off hurt. A lot. She could feel blood sticking to the fabric of her trousers.

'Where are you going?'

She had no idea. 'What's it to you?'

She couldn't go back to the party. But she couldn't go home, not yet. If ever. If she could ever work out where 'home' was. If she'd even had a home since she was twelve years old. The need to run was like a drug, pounding in her veins. She needed to be up high, moving fast, getting away from all this. She'd messed up so badly. She'd been in the same room as the one constable who was actually committed to finding her. She'd nearly got caught –

'Ida, wait!'

Clem grabbed Ida's wrist. She punched him. That hurt, too. He stumbled back into a dustbin, clattering to the floor. Rage mixed with pain across his face.

'What the hell was that for?!'

'Just piss off!'

'You piss off! I'm just trying to help, you're clearly in some sort of trouble –'

'And whose fault is that?' Ida yelled.

'How the hell should I know?' Clem yelled back, stumbling to his feet, 'I was in my smithy, minding my own business, and you fell off my roof! I come out here, and you're slumped over in the filth–'

'I tried to be nice,' Ida hissed, almost to herself. 'I tried to do something nice, for a friend, and look what happened. Stupid bar of chocolate, starting all this nonsense off…'

'Chocolate? What are you talking about?'

'…some stupid tit-for-tat of being nice, doing things

for people, where does it get you…'

It was suddenly very hard to breathe. Or focus. Or stand upright.

'Woah, woah, woah,' Clem said, suddenly holding her up by the shoulders. 'Ida, I think you need to come inside with me.'

'No… I need to go…'

'You're coming in with me to the smithy…'

'Let me go!'

'Ida,' Clem hissed, 'someone is going to think I'm trying to kidnap you.'

'I'd kill you first,' she spat in his face. He shook her shoulder none too gently.

'So get your arse in the smithy, sit down and have a bloody cup of water before you pass out.'

Clem's eyes were green. Like the gem. The gem she'd given to Casterbury to use to bring her down. To finally end The Rat Prince. Ida suddenly didn't want to think anymore. She let herself be led inside the smithy, as docile as a whipped horse.

It was warm inside the smithy. Not as oppressive as the last time she was here but comforting. Like being submerged into a cup of tea. Ida sunk down onto the chaise and could feel her eyes drooping before Clem had returned with her cup of water. He'd have a bruise on his cheek by the morning.

'Drink this,' he told her, 'and tell me what the hell is happening.'

'No.' Ida was so tired, all of a sudden. She didn't want

to talk or think. She felt defeated. Clem blew out a sigh.

'I've kind of guessed you're The Rat Prince, Ida. So, you might as well talk to me.'

Ida started, made to push past him, but Clem just laughed.

'What was I meant to do? Just assume that the famed criminal, known for his arrogance, suddenly changed his mind and decided to be charitable to a poor little jeweller like me? And that you happen to own a very true-to-life copy of his disguise when you toppled out of the sky tonight?'

Ida exhaled, sinking into the chaise further. She picked at the fabric of her trousers, now fused to her legs with blood.

'Don't tell anyone,' she muttered, instantly feeling ridiculous. She sounded like a bairn who'd been caught with their hand in the biscuit tin. Clem raised his hand solemnly, hooking his little finger under his thumb.

'Junior Inventor's Honour. So, did something go wrong, tonight?'

Ida told him everything. Everything. More than he needed to know. All about the job, and Casterbury, and how much she hated him. Everything about her mam dying, and Nan. Everything about Lucinda, and the brooch. About not sleeping, then feeling so lost and out of control ever since. She had no idea why she was telling him all of this. He could go to the   constables. But she knew he wouldn't. It felt like someone was pulling a rusting chain from her throat – painful, and strange – but afterwards, Ida's chest was emptier. Lighter. It had been years, after all.

Clem listened, nodding every so often. When she was finished, he took her cup from her, and re-filled it with water. As he sat next to her, his arm grazed hers. Ida found herself leaning against it.

'Since I worked something out about you,' he said, his hand resting on the side of her knee, 'I'll tell you something about me. I wasn't always the dashing, handsome, charming jeweller you see before you.'

'Who said you're handsome?' Ida said, weakly attempting a joke. Clem winked.

'C'mon, Ida. I own a mirror. But what I mean is: when I was a kid, I was really, really shy. I never felt right, in my own skin. My old skin. My old life, my old body, my old… everything. In fact, I felt like an imposter. So, I struck out on my own, and created myself over again. Dressed how I wanted, talked how I wanted, carried myself how I wanted. I even picked my own name! 'Clem', after Clementine Lepsum – because of my hair, you know? And I don't talk to my family anymore. They don't agree with who I am, now.'

'Who cares about them, then?' Ida said bluntly. 'They shouldn't be idiots.' Clem raised an eyebrow at her and huffed a small, ironic laugh through his nose.

'Yeah, you're right. How things are now – with my little shop and my adoring public with more money than sense – makes me so, so happy. My point is, we make ourselves into the people we want to be. Hang the rest, leave it all behind. It doesn't matter what your gran thinks of you, or some random posh git that's courting your boss.'

'And you couldn't give yourself this advice when Casterbury stole the gem from you in the first place?' Ida said, nudging Clem's leg with her own.   'I remember you being more than a little offended that he underestimated you.'

'I suppose. But it's easier to say this to you. Because you're brilliant, Ida. You really are.'

They held each other's gaze for a long, long moment. Then Clem blinked.

'I mean, you're the Rat Prince. You're a bloody legend. And you're going to get that gem back. But – if you don't mind me saying so – you can't do this one alone.'

As his grin became foxish, Ida noticed how white and sharp Clem's teeth were. How his eyes sparkled with mischief. It reminded her of the first time they'd met, back at the stall. Only now, she liked how it looked.

'So,' he said, tapping his chin, pretending to be deep in thought, 'This Kaelinite is incredibly powerful substance that could – hypothetically – be used to elevate the career of whichever enterprising soul happened to have it in their possession? And it just so happens that getting it back would be the perfect revenge on a man neither of us can stand?'

Ida couldn't help leaning in, grinning just as widely.

'Sounds about right.'

Clem nudged her ribs with his elbow.

'I want in.'

Chapter Twenty-Four

———

When Ida finally peeled off her trousers – after gingerly clambering back in through her mercifully wide-open bedroom window (something about her reckless mood tonight had finally turned out to be good luck, she supposed), she saw that her legs were indeed covered in blood. She softly dabbed at them with a washcloth until the worst of it was gone. Her left shin had a pretty bad bruise, and her right knee had a sizeable gash just under the kneecap. That would probably scar. As the adrenaline of her horrific night of work began to wear off, she realised it really hurt to flex that knee. She hadn't fallen off a roof since she was thirteen – how embarrassing. Even worse, it meant she couldn't run, couldn't jump. Whatever the plan ended up being, it wasn't going to happen for a week or two. The only trickery she'd be getting up to was wearing two pairs of stockings to hide the cuts from Lucinda. Luckily her arms were just scraped, probably nothing too noticeable.

Fortunately, Lucinda spent the last few days of the week being decidedly distracted. No, that wasn't exactly right. She was distant. One-word answers when Ida asked her questions about the house or her preferences for dinner that night, and certainly no chattering about exhibitions, or Clem, or even –

'Your Darling Devon is here!'

A disgustingly chipper Casterbury burst through the front door, caught Lucinda up in an embrace, dipped her and kissed her on the lips. Lucinda giggled shyly under his affections, then pushed him away lightly with the flat of a hand.

'No more, Devon, dear, I'm dizzy.'

Devon mashed one more kiss onto her cheek before releasing her, and Ida swore she saw Lucinda's hand swipe across her skin. Maybe she was protecting a new rouge? She must be; she had excused herself to go shopping that week, instead of sending Ida. And as far as Ida knew she was still smitten with her consort; no shouting matches, no dramatic displays of fury or remorse. Devon monologued as he strutted around the house, acting as if he owned it all already.

'…just a little event with a few associates, just showing off a little business venture I've been working on. Something that I think this city sorely needs, what with all these reprobates coming out of the woodwork in recent years – people who, instead of finding honest, productive work, would rather steal from hardworking citizens like us.'

Ida felt slightly sick.

'And of course,' Casterbury continued, making his way around Lucinda's drawing room, pawing at vases and notecards and other items that Ida had spent the better part of her morning rearranging, 'there will be time for socialising. A little music, a tipple or two. And perhaps,' he said, winking, 'a little personal announcement? From us?'

Lucinda blinked. Ida blinked.

Here we go. Goodbye, Rat Prince.

'Devon,' Lucinda tentatively began, straightening a small sketch of Eloise and Daniel as children that she kept on her letter-writing desk, 'that sounds…lovely. But I really think that we should –'

'Talk about it over dinner? Capital idea, my darling! Let me organise a luncheon at my abode. We can discuss any arrangements and formalities then, with food in our stomachs and wine in our glasses. I shall write to you with a time to be ready – until then, my sweet, I must away, business is calling, goodbye my angel, goodbye…'

As Ida limped behind Casterbury and helped him with his coat, Casterbury's arm wrapped around her waist – just for a second – and squeezed.

'I'm sure you're ready for there to be a man about the house, Ida,' he murmured, a laugh bubbling in his voice like tar. 'See you soon.'

Ida wanted to slam the door behind him – or, better yet, slam it repeatedly onto his…

'Ida? Finish tidying the drawing room, then I'd like the bathrooms scrubbed. Please.'

When Ida entered the drawing room, Lucinda was looking at the sketch of Eloise and Daniel. Two dark, curly heads, almost identical – charcoal in the picture, rich brown in real life – beamed up at her. Eloise was sitting like a grown-up little lady, while Daniel had his arm looped around her, grinning at the artist, showing off a gap in his front teeth. Lucinda didn't look up as Ida entered the room and picked up her duster from the arm of the brocade chaise longue. No chatter, no conversation.

'I always liked that sketch,' Ida offered, as she began cleaning the nooks and crannies of the old bronze quill-dipper on Lucinda's writing desk. 'How old were they?'

'Eloise was eight,' Lucinda said, after a long pause, 'so Daniel was six. Please don't leave your dusters on the furniture, Ida. It's unseemly.'

'Yes ma'am.'

Lucinda stayed in the drawing room, looking at pictures and old letters as Ida attempted to work around her. It was awkward. It had never been awkward between them before. Strange, but not awkward. Lucinda was an oversharing, clingy, talkative woman. Normally, anyway. As Ida moved to leave and take her work to another room, Lucinda spoke again, still with her back to her maid.

'We were never blessed with children. Jonathan and I. And so, we spoiled those two so much when they were young. Toys, chocolates… they both knew they could always come to their Aunt Lucinda and Uncle Jonathan. To have little ones running around the house again, bringing so much life and laughter and… it's one of life's true gifts. I want that more than anything in this world. Do you understand my meaning?'

Ida stood in the doorway for a long moment. She could reach out to her mistress. She could touch her arm, tell her… what? What on earth could a nineteen-year-old maid tell an heiress to make her life better? Nothing, that was what. Lucinda probably wasn't even talking to Ida directly. Better to just walk away, leave her to her thoughts. Perhaps that was even kinder than trying to drag it out of her. It could be hard to talk about your family. Ida had almost never done such a thing, and talking to Clem about it all had felt horrifically awkward. She remembered that rusting chain feeling, the heaviness of speaking about her pain, and decided to spare Lucinda that feeling.

Look at you, Ida Finn. Being considerate of others.

She scrubbed both bathrooms until they shone, polished the banisters, and was about to tackle the herculean effort of stripping, washing and changing the bedsheets in all the guest bedrooms when she heard Lucinda speaking again. It sounded like she was talking to someone, sounding much cheerier than she had, which was a good sign.

'…upstairs, somewhere. She never mentioned looking for extra work to me…'

'…just an idea. I promised her it wouldn't interfere with her day job, Ms. Belmonte…'

Was that Edith?

'Ida! Ida, your little friend has been sent from the Acutus, to talk to you about the serving position?'

…what?

Ida leaned over the bannister to see Lucinda and Edith in the foyer. Edith was wearing her Acutus uniform, wringing her cloth cap in her hands, slightly uncomfortable in her surroundings.

'I've never been in such a beautiful home, Ms. Belmonte,' she was saying. 'it's so much bigger than my little house near the river.' Lucinda was tittering and saying 'oh, do call me Lucinda' and very clearly trying to resist touching Edith's hair. They looked up together and spied Ida. Edith flashed a wide, toothsome smile in her direction.

'Ida!' she chirped loudly, 'Cook sent me to talk to you about the serving position!'

Ida tilted her head in confusion. Edith guffawed, and beckoned her down, laughing almost in Lucinda's face.

'You remember, silly! I take on little jobs every now and then as a serving girl, Ms. Belmonte – Lucinda, sorry. Just helping out at parties and functions our patrons throw. I was at Lord Casterbury's house just the other night, actually – helping out with a function…'

'Oh, really dear? What a small world Loxport can be!'

Edith's gaze slowly, deliberately, turned back to skewer Ida's. She suddenly felt like a piece of bait in the aquariums at the Schuyler that had suddenly been thrown into a tank with an extra-friendly shark.

'Yes, it is. And I know Ida is always looking for ways to make a little extra money.'

Chapter Twenty-Five

———

Lucinda let Ida take her lunch break slightly early to talk with Edith about the 'serving position.' Edith followed Ida up the stairs into the servant's quarters. Ida opened her bedroom door, and Edith strode in without saying thank you. As the door closed with a soft click, Edith spun and smacked Ida across the head with her cloth cap.

'Oi!' Ida yelped. Edith swung again. This time Ida grabbed the cap and wrenched it away. 'What the hell's the matter with you –'

'What's the matter with me?!' Edith shrieked. Ida lunged for the deadbolt on her door.

'Keep your voice down,' she hissed. 'Lucinda –'

'Lucinda?' Edith's whisper was shrill; she sounded like a tire on a Horseless running out of air. 'Lucinda?! You want to think yourself lucky I don't march out there and tell Lucinda exactly what you've been up to…'

'Edith, I have no idea what –'

'I saw you, Ida.' Edith snatched her cloth cap up from the floor and brandished it in Ida's face. 'I saw you crouching on Devon Casterbury's landing like… like some sort of goblin.'

Well, what could she say to that? Except for;

'... ah.'

'I should have known,' Edith whimpered to herself, knotting her hands in her hair in frustration. 'I should have known when you stole an entire boat, calmly as you like. Who steals a boat? Apart from wretched, immoral... indecent criminals!'

'...well, I suppose you're right.'

Edith's face darkened.

'Is that all you've got to say to me?'

What else was there? Ida thought for a moment. 'Um... how did you recognise me?'

Edith's mouth fell open in a perfect O. 'How... how did I recognise you?'

Her voice plummeted into the deepest Loxportian accent Ida had ever heard as she advanced, her hair trembling with rage.

'Because, y'stupid idiot, I'd like to think I'd know me best mate when she's standin' reet in front of me, wearin' a pair of stupid goggles on her heed!'

'...did you just say I was your best mate?' Ida stammered.

'I might have,' Edith hissed. 'I'm very angry and can't remember what I said just now.'

'And my goggles aren't stupid, anyway. They're a highly sophisticated piece of equipment.'

'Ah, c'mon, Ida,' Edith shook her head so hard her hair hit her in the eyes. 'They look like you've got two glass beer bottles strapped to your head.'

The fight paused as Edith scraped her hair back from

her face, forcing it back under her cap.

'How stupid are you?' she said, calmer than she was but no less upset. 'You'll get caught one day, 'cos of your own greed, and selfishness, and 'cos you hate Devon bloody Casterbury that much you're willing to stalk him…'

Ida felt herself puff up like an angry cat.

'You think I do all this for Casterbury?'

'Why else would you?'

'Oh, because I have absolutely no life outside of that pompous… you know why I do it? You want to know what I do with the money I get?'

'I don't care what you spend your dirty money on,' Edith sniffed, folding her arms. Ida took her by the forearm and dragged her to the wardrobe in the   corner of the room.

'No, no – if you're my 'best friend',' Ida said, yanking open the doors, 'you should know what the stupid, greedy Rat Prince is really like.'

She gestured with a flourish. Lining the floor of the wardrobe were around twenty coffee cans, all full of money. Some, near the back, were organised into Athenas and Hermes. The later ones, close to the front, were a hodgepodge of coins; some shiny, some dull and worn.

'That,' Ida whispered fiercely in Edith's ear, 'is my earnings. Everything I earn as a maid goes on food and clothing – oh, and a bag of sugared almonds once a week. How indulgent. This 'dirty money',' Ida said, crouching down and plunging her hand into a can, letting the coins slip through her fingers, 'is the leftovers.

After I pay for my grandmother's bills, and her food, and everything else she takes without as much as a thank you. And I only keep doing it, only keep in contact with the horrible old bat, because my mam did it. Before she died. Oh, and because if I don't, she might dob me in to stupid bloody Thomas and Doreen. Whoever they are.'

'Ida, I'm sorry…' Edith began.

'In fact, that's why I steal, you know? Because of my mam; she taught me all of this! How to hide my accent, how to get a job in a big house, how to steal and not get caught. Mam was so proud of me! But she never got around to teaching me what to do with all the money I earned. Sorry; stole. Not like I can get a fancy house, is it? Not like I can buy my way into being a lady, like Lucinda. Get my own maids, give someone else a pittance to live on. Not with this accent, not with this education, this breeding. So, what's it for? But I can't stop. If I stop – well, she's gone, isn't she? My mam's gone for good. Properly dead. That's your answer, there; being The Rat Prince is the only way I can feel close to my dead mam and forget that I'll be pressing Lucinda Belmonte's petticoats every day for the rest of my life. Happy now?'

That was a lot. Suddenly exhausted and feeling the pain in her leg, Ida sat heavily on the bed and sunk her head into her hands. That awkward, painful, lighter feeling was back. Ida had barely ever given the feelings she'd had about money a thought before, and now they were out in the open. Like when the smoke from a housefire finally bursts through a window and fills up the street.

For a moment, the only noise was the sound of her breath, cupped between her palms. Then, Edith's hand slid onto her knee.

'Ida… I'm sorry. I didn't know any of that. And I'm sorry I made you think I didn't care about you. Because I do, I promise. I'm only angry because I don't want to see you get arrested. That might feel odd, and hard to understand, but it's true.'

It was purely coincidence that Ida leaned in as Edith's arms wrapped around her shoulders. Honestly. Her own arms untangling themselves to hug Edith back, however, was intentional.

'I didn't tell them anything,' Edith said into Ida's shoulder. 'When they came after you at the party. I just said I was seeing things in the shadows.'

'Thank you, Edie. That wasn't a good night, for me.'

After a long moment, Edith moved away to push her hair out of her eyes again.

'So why The Rat Prince?' she asked.

'What?'

'Why did you call yourself The Rat Prince? Was it some sort of, I dunno, pot-shot at the lords and ladies that you're stealing from, or…?'

Ida snorted a laugh.

'You think I gave myself a criminal alter ego? No, they –' gesturing out the window at the rest of the city – 'gave me that name. I was sixteen, I think? Fifteen, nearly sixteen. And they finally cottoned on that all these thefts had the same mastermind behind them. Some reporter at the Loxport Express came up with it on their tea break, or something. It never even occurred to them that I could be a girl, for God's sake. I just went with it; another layer of protection between me and the constables.'

'It just seems too dangerous,' Edith said, resting her chin on the top of Ida's head. 'Would you actually want some serving work on the side? I could talk to Cook, I'm sure she wouldn't mind, and the hosts would appreciate the help. I'm working a few parties at Casterbury's house for my sins, and the money isn't bad… what is it?'

Ida had sat up straight, dislodging her friend with a jolt. She stared at Edith with wide eyes, stock still. Edith shifted in her seat. 'That's the same look you gave me in the boat,' she said warily. 'Are you free next Wednesday?' Ida asked.

'…yes. Well, after I make breakfast, and make sure Kate's alright, and do a few things around the house—'

'Good,' Ida said. There's someone I want you to meet.'

Chapter Twenty-Six

———

'Oh, I know where we're going!' Edith said, as Ida led her down the uneven cobbles towards Sixmith Street. 'The little shop with the blue sign, next to the shop that sells vases that look like–'

'Yeah.'

'And you put the flowers in the–'

'Yes, Edith. That's the shop. Now please stop talking about it.'

'My uncle's friend runs that pottery place. Really nice man. Knowledgeable.'

'That's great, Edie. Thank you for making this day as awkward as possible.'

'You love me really.'

Ida had managed to scribble a note to Clem earlier in the week, telling him they were coming. Lucinda had barely noticed when she asked for a spare scrap of paper, let alone what it was for. She'd simply eaten her breakfast, smiled weakly in Ida's direction, then wandered off into the house to read. Ida hoped Lucinda wasn't pregnant. She wasn't sure what the etiquette was for widows, but in her part of town there'd be a solid screaming match, followed by a night of 'wetting the baby's head' with whiskey, and a quick appointment at the church the next morning. None of which she was prepared for. Plus, the idea of another Casterbury in the world set her teeth on edge.

Clem opened the door on Ida's second knock. He wasn't as sweaty as the first time she'd seen inside his home, nor as snappish as the second. He answered the door with a flourish. The bruise on his cheekbone was fading to a yellowish tinge.

'Welcome, old friends and new,' he drawled, 'to my humble abode. You must be Edith,' he said, sweeping her hand up in a firm handshake. 'You'll have to forgive my surprise – when Ida mentioned in her letter that she was bringing a friend, I thought to myself Clem, my boy, surely you have misread.'

'Alright, very funny. Can we go inside now?' Ida muttered.

'Because, my dear Clem, the Ida Finn you know and adore so much is a lone wolf. As solitary as an oyster, as deep as the depths…'

'Get inside the smithy, you absolute lunatic.'

Ida shoved a chuckling Clem none too gently against the doorjamb, and strode inside. Clem shut the door behind them. Ida looked over her shoulder at him, and he winked at her before jogging into the workshop.

'Let me just grab my notes.'

As he disappeared, Edith spun on her heel to face Ida.

'Nice,' she mouthed silently, pointing a finger in Clem's direction and pantomiming… blowing on something hot? Ida wasn't sure. She shrugged blankly, and Edith waved her hands dismissively. 'Spoilsport,' she muttered.

'Right,' Clem said, returning with a leather-bound journal and fistful of pencils, 'before we start, can I offer you both refreshments? Water, tea… erm… a different type of tea?'

'I don't think I've ever been at a gathering of criminals where I was offered a cup of tea.' Ida sighed.

'Well,' Clem sniffed, 'we are a civilized bunch. I might go to prison for aiding and abetting, but no-one can say I'm not a good host.'

Edith drew her legs underneath her. 'Ha… yes… prison…' Her brow creased as she played thoughtfully with a curl of hair. Ida knew what she was thinking. Kate. She had someone that needed her, someone she actually loved. And still she wanted to help. The other shoe had dropped, she'd realised the stakes, and she wasn't getting up and running screaming from the room. She must have some faith in me, at least.

'We aren't going to prison,' Ida said, untangling Edith's hand from where it was becoming knotted in her hair. 'Ask me how I know.'

'How?' Edith said.

Ida smirked. 'Because,' she replied, her voice growing lower and raspier, tilting her head to the side like watchful predator, 'you've got The Rat Prince on your side. And this time, he's not going in alone.'

'Oooh,' Clem shuddered gleefully, destroying the atmosphere. Idiot.

'Now, here's the plan...'

Over the past week, The Rat Prince had gone quiet. Not so quiet as to be suspicious – he still found himself the new owner of a pocket watch or three from just wandering about at the right time of night and quite literally bumping into the right sort of sot – but there were no break-ins, no burglaries. Ida focused on getting the flexibility back in her leg. She started off slowly, hopping from the top of her wardrobe to the bed and back, climbing out her window and onto the roof of Lucinda's house as many times as she could in a night without being seen. But there was this itch in the back of her mind, this need she had to be up high and moving fast. She overexerted herself a few times and her stiff legs paid the price the next morning, but that first time she leapt from a rooftop, feeling the ground beneath her feet shift and fall away, only to catch her again on the other side, was too wonderful to wait for.

In the meantime, Casterbury called upon Lucinda for their candlelit supper together. When she returned, she was even quieter than she had been previously: she simply handed Ida her fur coat, mumbled something about not needing a bath tonight, prepared herself for bed, and then disappeared.

Later that night, Ida had silently crept downstairs into the kitchen and cracked open the back door. Edith was standing there, hugging herself.

'I'm bloody freezing,' she whined by way of greeting.

'Do you want to come in?' Ida asked. 'If you're quiet,

and don't touch anything…'

'Nah, it's ok. I have to keep a watch on this one…'

At the end of the lane, yawning dramatically, was a young girl. She had the same round face and freckles as Edith, but her hair was more brassy than red, and straight as an arrow.

'You must be Kate,' Ida called softly. Kate saluted, standing as straight as a constable.

'Ignore her, she's weird,' Edith said.

'Why'd you bring her along? It's the middle of the night.'

'Um… exactly?' Edith looked at Ida as if she were an idiot. 'I'm not leaving her in the house alone, Ida.'

'Why? The most notorious criminal in Loxport is right here.'

Edith rolled her eyes affectionately.

'Idiot. Anyway. So, Casterbury's little dinner with your boss. God, that was an awkward supper. He asked her why she thought he'd invited her around, and she said…'

'Never mind that, Edie. What did he say about the investments?'

'I'm getting to that. He has teamed up with the constables, like you thought. He said something about using a new resource –'

'The Kaelinite.'

'…to power a kind of alarm system. He called it the Sentinel. He's going to get his house kitted out with this thing first, so he can show off how clever it is. He got the blueprints out to show her, and by this point you could tell she wanted to go home. But I grabbed a fancy bottle of wine I'd snagged from the Acutus and pretended it was a gift from the club.'

'So of course they had to sample it. We'll make a crook out of you yet, Webb.'

'Ha. As I was pouring, I had a sneaky peek. He just kept talking, barely even noticing me, the massive   pillock. It looked like a lantern, with the gem inside, and a, like, screen in front of it. Made of parchment or something. And if you walked in front of it, the gem sent a signal to a bell inside the house. It's all connected with these thin pipes.'

'Like a guard outside the house at all times,' Ida mused. 'Thanks, Edie. I'll get the intel to Clem and see what he thinks. Maybe he can do a walk-by while we're at work sometime.'

'Edith,' a voice at Ida's elbow whined, 'when can we go home? I'm tired, and it's bloody freezing.'

'We're going now, my sweetness. Get you all tucked up in bed with your dolly,' Edith said, crouching down to hug her sister. She planted a smacker of a kiss on the side of Kate's head, and the girl twisted away with playful disgust.

'Edith! I'm twelve, I'm too old for dollies. Or kisses.'

'You will never be too old for my kisses,' Edith swore. 'I best get her home, Ida. Is any of that helpful?'

'It's a start. Cheers, Edie.'

Ida watched the pair as they walked towards the end of Juniper Avenue. Edith had her arm around the small of her sister's back, and Kate leaned her head on her sister's shoulder as they turned the corner and vanished from view. It was only then Ida realised that Kate was the same age she was when she started her burglary career. She gave herself twenty seconds to feel the ache in her chest, ponder on its meaning (Jealousy? Nostalgia? A mix of the two?) before creeping back upstairs to cram in three hours of sleep before her day began anew. She was beginning to sleep a little better, these days.

Chapter Twenty-Seven

———

That week, Ida leapt at the chance to run errands. It was a chance to give her leg a little exercise during the workday, and it got her away from Lucinda's unsettling quietness. Her wicker basket knocked against her good leg as she walked, filled with Lucinda's order of letter-writing paper, a new set of ostrich-feather quills, and a baker's dozen of Lucinda's favourite toffee shortbread. Only the essentials, of course. Just a set of shoes to collect from the cobblers. She'd probably even have time for an excursion along the River Lox, for the extra legwork, before she was expected back.

Who knows, I might even find that boat, Ida thought. Now that's an idea – just get in a boat and sail away from Loxport, leave it all behind. That Malko woman does it all the time, how hard can it be?

'Oi! Get back here!'

Someone dashed into the road in front of Ida – straight into the path of an old-fashioned carriage. The horse reared up, and the lad crumpled to the floor, hands above his head. Ida leapt to the side before she had time to think and grabbed the horse's reins, pulling him back a little from the body in his path. Ida might be a master criminal, but she didn't want to watch someone get trampled to death. Besides, imagine explaining the bloodstains on her dress to Lucinda.

'Hey, hey,' she said, trying to mimic the tone she'd heard used by stablehands at the place by the Lord and Horse, 'Shush now, it's alright laddie.'

The horse turned towards her, tipping the carriage ever so slightly. He was still tossing his head, eyes wide and scared, but at least he hadn't killed anyone. As the driver thanked Ida and steered the carriage back on track, two constables ran into its path.

'Move on! Move on, now!' one yelled, waving his arms in the horse's face as if he could understand him.

'We're trying sir,' the driver said through gritted teeth. 'Just wanna go pick up my employer, don't want no bother.'

'Well… don't forget it,' the constable said, glaring meaningfully. The driver blinked, then clicked his tongue and moved his carriage off. In the meantime, the other constable had grabbed the boy in the road and wrenched his head up by the hair.

'Tryin' to get away, eh, Reggie? Got something to hide?'

Reggie?

Oh no.

'I didn't do anything, man!' Reggie Powell snapped, trying to twist away like a rabbit in a snare. The constable had him in a tight grip and shook him hard to make him shut up.

'Aye, aye. I'm sure. Bet you had nothing to do with the break-in on Gryffin Avenue this morning? The vandalism?

I think the description might match you, don'tcha think so, Mick?'

'Aye,' the other constable sniggered. 'Think you should come in for questioning, Reggie. Maybe your dad can come down and bail you out, and we could have a chat with him too…'

'Oh, Reggie!' Ida called, flapping her hand in a wave. 'How did your meeting go at the shipyard?'

The three men turned to look at her as if they'd only just realised she was there. Ida supposed that when you dressed in a maid's uniform, you don't really exist; not until someone needs something of you, anyway.

Reggie squinted at her, shaking his head. Oh, for God's sake, Reg, help me out, here…

'Do you think Odessa Malko will take you aboard? Oh, it'd be so exciting to work on one of her ships! Seeing the world, having adventures with a famous scientist…'

Lord in Heaven, she'd been possessed by Edith. Ida forced her voice to become as high and as bubbly as her friend's, all the while making unblinking eye contact with Reg until, finally, the Hermes dropped.

'Uh…aye, aye!' he said. 'She seems… dead canny. Could be good, aye.'

It wasn't the best acting in the world. But coupled with Ida's expensive looking uniform and her name-dropping of a famous scientist, it was enough to loosen the grip the constable had on Reggie's arm.

'Tryin' to move up in the world, are you?' one growled

sarcastically. Reggie had the good sense to nod and say nothing.

'Can I please look after him from here, sirs?' Ida continued. 'We were going to go for a cup of tea to celebrate…'

The constables looked at each other for a long beat, before letting Reggie go. As soon as he darted for the pavement though, the other constable – Mick – grabbed him by the scruff.

'Soon enough, Powell,' he snarled, 'you're not going to be able to get away from us. Just wait and see what happens, my son.'

He shoved Reggie away and the two constables marched off. Reggie stumbled to the floor, tripping over the curb as he went. Ida knelt beside him.

'Y'alright, Reg?' she heard herself say, her voice becoming her own again. She was so used to making her voice lower and harsher – she'd never tried a higher pitch before. It was odd. Reggie looked up at her sharply.

'I didn't need any help,' he muttered. 'Cheers, like, but I didn't need a stranger to help me out.'

As he shrugged off his embarrassment and barged his way back into the Loxport crowd, Ida realised how far Casterbury's plans – these Sentinel things – could reach; far beyond The Rat Prince. How much Loxport could be shaped by one man and his pride.

Chapter Twenty-Eight

———

'So how are you sleeping, Ida?'

Clem glanced sideways at Ida as they and Edith walked around Big Pond Park together. Ida insisted they meet up and just go for a slow, meandering walk on her day off. Purely for the sake of her leg, of course.

'… fine?' Ida answered. Clem raised an eyebrow at Edith, who walked beside him, arms linked together. The two of them were forming a cosy little twosome these days, it was quite disconcerting.

'Are you sure?' Clem asked. 'Feeling well rested? Not having any strange nightmares about, I don't know… deep-seated fears, old wounds from your past?'

'No. Not for a while. So, I thought we could do once around Big Pond, then head to the Boathouse for scones.'

'Sleeping better since, I don't know. A few days after giving up the Kaelinite?'

'I suppose,' Ida conceded warily. Clem and Edith shared a knowing look. 'Right,' Ida said, 'something is obviously up, and the two of you are going to tell me before I take back my offer of scones.'

'So,' Clem said, clapping his hands together, 'Kaelinite has somewhat of a reputation. Turns out there are myths about it that date back hundreds of years, when the first explorers charted the darkest corners of the world. It's been said to emit great power, easy to manipulate to your whims. At a price.'

'And how do you know all this?' Ida asked. Clem stepped in front of her and squatted down to her eye level, holding both her hands in one of his own. Ida stared down at them as if he'd put them in a vice.

'Now, Ida,' Clem said, in his most syrupy-sweet tone. 'There's this new form of technology; it's really cutting edge, so you might not have heard of it. It's called a 'book'? Do you think you can pronounce that?'

'Shut up,' Ida growled, as she attempted to pull herself free. Clem, with all his strength from the smithy, merely pulled her along for a few steps, walking backwards while holding her hands.

'Well, trying to find a learned gent to tell me about it didn't work, not even with eyelashes as long and beguiling as mine. So instead, I charmed the librarian at one of the smaller universities, and she let a lowly pleb like me borrow some books, to further my knowledge and grow my mind and such. And wouldn'tcha know it, one had a whole chapter on The Lightning Stone. Otherwise known as Kaelinite.'

'"After the Lightning bares its teeth, the darkness swallows you whole,"' Edith quoted from behind them. Ida looked over her shoulder.

'And how do you know about this?'

'Clem invited me over for tea so we could talk.'

'I thought I was meant to be the leader of this band of criminals.'

'We never discussed that. What we did discuss was your lack of sleep.'

That was when Ida wrenched her hands away from Clem's. 'You've been talking about me behind my back?' That black tar feeling swept through her bloodstream. 'What have you been saying? I can do this job, you know; just because I was tired, and… and weak, for a while…'

'Oh, Ida.' Edith stepped around Clem, batting him away like a fly. 'We never thought you were weak.'

'But I was,' Ida said, almost crossing her arms petulantly before remembering she wasn't a child anymore. Who were they to tell her she wasn't being dramatic and senseless and useless when she knew she was? 'You don't have to pretend I wasn't. I made reckless, stupid decisions like stealing that boat, and stalking Casterbury, and…'

'This is what I'm trying to tell you, you goose,' Clem interrupted. 'Kaelinite gives you night terrors. It gives the person who owns it all this power, but it also shows you all your deepest fears, all the most awful things in your past, and makes you unable to sleep. And once you can't sleep, you're susceptible to acting irrationally. It stains your mind for days after the last time you touch it. It's a cursed jewel. I'd love to know how it ended up in my shipment of Peridot.'

'But luckily for us,' Edith continued, 'one of the things you consider to be irrational is opening up. Letting us in. Letting us care about you. And that's a really, really good thing.'

'Because then we can pool our knowledge to get the Kaelinite back,' Ida finished, nodding to herself. Edith and Clem shared one last aggravating, secret look between themselves.

'And because we get to know you.' Edith said   quietly. Clem shoved his hands in his pockets and pursed his lip. If Ida didn't know better, she'd say he almost looked shy. But that couldn't be right.

'Clem,' Edith asked, clearing her throat a little, 'tell her your theory about the Sentinel.'

'Ah, yes. Right. So.' Clem spun on his heel and strode off in the direction of the teahouse, 'Essentially, if everyone in Loxport has a piece of Kaelinite in their homes, everyone – at least the people who can afford to keep their homes and businesses Rat Prince-free – will start having night terrors. Everyone in Loxport will be tired, constantly dwelling on their worst fears, and subject to, as you put it Ida,' he said, whirling and making air quotes with his fingers, '"reckless, stupid decisions." Thus, crumbling the city we know around us into an exhausted, paranoid mess.'

'And,' Edith added, squeezing Ida's shoulder, 'if a lot of Kaelinite is going into people's homes to protect them from the Rat Prince, just think what these people will do when they catch him.'

Ah.

Ida pondered this for a long while as they walked. Big Pond Park did look lovely; full of happy, well-rested people, their minds on nothing more terrifying than getting the soles of their shoes dirty.

'Well,' she said with a grim smile, 'we'd better get it back, then. Clem, does that mean you're ready for your little mission?'

'Ready as I'll ever be, mon capitan. But first…' Clem pointed forward with all the flourish of a general   going off to war, 'I demand scones!'

Chapter Twenty-Nine

———

'Ida, will you get the door, please?'

Of course I will. It's literally part of my job.

Clem stood on the doorstep. He was dressed quite smartly; button-up navy shirt and a bottle-green waistcoat under a dark grey peacoat, all of which made his shock of ginger hair stand out even more so. Nothing he was wearing looked particularly expensive, but the confidence with which he wore it put Devon Casterbury's peacocking to shame. He would look at home with Daniel, lounging about in the park, writing poetry about the stars or something. His velocipede leaned against the garden wall, attracting disapproving stares from the neighbours.

'Good morning, miss,' he said. 'Is the lady of the house at home? I have finished her commission for a...'

'Oh, Clem, dear! What a wonderful surprise!'

Lucinda hurtled down the corridor from the drawing room like a locomotive. Ida stepped nimbly to one side as the two embraced. As Lucinda pulled back from the hug, she was grinning. For the first time in ages, she was showing an emotion other than vague sadness. Interesting.

'Do you have it?' she said, pressing his hands in her

own. Clem winked at her with that tongue-clicking noise. He seemed to enjoy doing that. Ida hadn't worked out yet if it was annoying or endearing.

'I wouldn't disappoint my favourite customer! Now, I know you wanted earrings to match the Bismuth you bought from the exhibition, but I thought; Clem, she needs a full set. So, I have this bracelet to show you, absolutely no pressure to commit...'

'Ida, darling, bring us some iced water and lemon. Clem, can I offer you something sweet while we chat? I have some delightful evronberry tart, if you would like.'

'That sounds delightful. Quick-sharp now, Ida, darling.'

Clem's eyebrows arched as he spoke, barely containing his mirth at getting to order her about. Ida turned on her heel and disappeared into the kitchen.

Approximately two hours or thirty years later, when the two emerged giggling and plotting together from the drawing room, Ida was ready.

'Can I give Mr. Magnesan his coat?' she offered through gritted teeth.

'Why thank you, Ida darling,' Clem replied, slipping his arms through the sleeves as she held his coat open. His right hand touched hers, just for a second, and a tightly-rolled up scroll of paper slotted between her forefinger and thumb.

'Does Ida have a moment to step outside with me, Ms. Belmonte?' Clem asked, shrugging on his coat. 'I'd like to have a little chat with her. See if I can't persuade her to spend her Hermes on upgrading her own necklace to a matching set.'

Ida's fingers went to the pearl around her neck, hidden under her uniform. What was he doing? She had the note, there was nothing left to say, surely? Lucinda looked at Ida quizzically.

'I'm sorry, Mr. Magnesan,' Ida replied, 'but I have a lot to do today. Perhaps next time?'

Clem's face fell, just for a split second. Then he covered it up with a smile and a nod to Lucinda.

'Until then, ladies: adieu, adieu…'

Lucinda was underfoot for the rest of the day. She wasn't entirely back to normal, but Ida was shown the Bismuth earrings she'd bought from Clem at least five times and heard every detail of the bracelet she was considering adding to the collection. 'You have to reel them in slowly, Ida,' she said, nibbling on the last of the evronberry tart. 'Men relish the chase!'

By the time she was alone, Ida's head was pounding. Still, she couldn't rest yet. She needed to know what Clem knew. She locked herself in her lavatory, unrolled the note, and read:

Ignescent, Ignoble Ida,

Took a little walk, as you recommended. Happened to stroll past the abode of a mutual friend of ours, who has had some rather marvellous remodelling done to his home. We simply must journey together to see it very soon.

I can't think how to write this next part in code. The

Sentinel is about the size of a shoebox, with canvas stretched over it. The gem is inside, or rather a shard of it, emitting a light. The gem must be set up to some sort of spindle inside that turns it and registers any motion in front of it as unwanted. Pass in front of the canvas, anywhere in range of the light, an alarm sounds inside the house, and you are caught. Won't stop talking about it with his neighbours, proud as punch.

God, he looks knackered – kept rubbing his eyes and yawning, which I was brought up to think wasn't very polite. But what do we know, eh?

Your Captivating, Calculating
Clem
xx

The 'xx' at the end looked rushed next to Clem's handsome, looping writing. Odd. Ida rolled the note back up and slipped it under her mattress as she left to finish her duties for the evening.

After Lucinda had gone to bed, Ida changed into her trousers and tunic. She skipped across the city, with no real end destination in mind. She needed to stretch her legs, and her mind.

She'd ignored her cubby holes for a while now. Ah, well. After what she was planning, she'd be able to take any job she wanted. She'd be free. Professionally, at least. And she guessed that any excuse to be out of the house would be welcome soon enough, when Casterbury had made his little 'personal announcement'.

Ida found herself perched in the crow's nest of an unfinished vessel in the shipyards: a grand looking thing, probably meant for some rich explorer to go out into the wilds of the world and find adventure, knowledge, and riches. After the building crews had all gone home for the night, the shipyards could be a relatively peaceful place to come and think. She felt like the kittiwakes she loved so much – high up, free, and safe, at least for a little while.

Water lapped around the boat, before curling back to flow out into the North Sea beyond. Ida dangled her legs into the space below her and let her mind wander.

It was probably time to admit to herself that she had friends. Two whole people now knew her secrets, and neither of them had gone running to the constables, or Lucinda. Instead, they had both plunged themselves into a heist without a second thought, following her lead. That must account for something. Unless they were both running an incredibly long and convoluted con.

If Casterbury's Sentinel was a success there was no way he'd stop there. Patents for products that hadn't even been invented yet swirled in Ida's head like paper snowflakes, threatening to turn into an avalanche. He had to fail. It didn't matter if Lucinda was prepared to settle for someone unworthy of her and bear his blonde, posh children; Casterbury, and all his little ideas for security, were going down.

Chapter Thirty

————

Lucinda Belmonte still had the rosy complexion of a teenager, but the corners of her eyes seemed pinched, and the ghosts of worry lines danced over her forehead.

'You look lovely, ma'am,' Ida offered. Lucinda didn't turn away from her mirror; simply nodded and continued to fuss with her hair. Tonight was the big showcase of Devon Casterbury's latest passion project, and Lucinda was expected to attend. More than attend: she was one of the exhibits. And, once she was gone, Ida's plan would come to fruition.

A few days prior, Ida had watched from a rooftop as Clem strode across Devon Casterbury's threshold.

'Good morning, Lord Casterbury, I'm sure you remember me – Clem Magnesan, favoured jeweller of your beautiful paramour, Ms. Belmonte.'

'Quite. But I must ask what this is in aide of.'

'Of course, sir; a very pertinent, intelligent question, sir. Ms. Belmonte wrote to me just yesterday morning asking me if I would pop in and see you at your beautiful abode and – oh, my! What a magnificent alarm! Is that the coming of the Rapture, or merely a thousand cowbells?'

'A new invention,' Casterbury had sniffed. 'State of the art, scientific breakthrough, you know. Step out the way, boy.'

He flipped some switch inside his hallway, and the cacophony stopped.

'Anyway: Lucinda?'

'Yes, our dear mutual friend informed me that there may be a... ahem... a certain happy event soon enough? And she wanted me to go over the styles, the cuts and the facets that she prefers in her jewellery, you know these things are incredibly important to a lady, happiest day of her life and all that. Won't take a second sir, I assure you. What absolutely stunning wallpaper you have, sir, absolutely masterful, now the lady does enjoy a subtle band with a Marquise cut...'

So there was a disabling point by the door. Ida watched as light after light bloomed and dimmed in Casterbury's home: Clem striding around Casterbury's home, looking for the rest of the Kaelinite. When he found the room, it was being kept in – top floor, back room, with the red silk curtains – he kept the lamp burning as he took his leave, roughly fifteen minutes later, no doubt talking the entire time. Ida almost pitied Casterbury.

'Excellent talking to you, sir, an absolute treat to see inside such a wonderful home, Ms. Belmonte is going to be a very, very happy lady, all the best to you both, sir...'

'I have no idea what she sees in him,' Ida had said earlier, as the pair worked out their plan. Ida sprawled across Clem's chaise with her weekly bag of treats, while Clem perched on the battered old coffee table beside her.

'What; you don't believe in true love?' Clem said, snatching an almond from the bag and popping it into his mouth.

'Hey!' Ida pulled her bag away as Clem laughed to himself triumphantly. 'Get your own sweets.'

'I am the Rat Prince now,' Clem crowed, rising from his seat, hands on hips.

'They'd be mopping you up from the cobbles by the weekend,' Ida replied.

'Don't fuss, you miser: if you share I'll pay you back. So?'

'So, what?' Ida asked, begrudgingly holding her almonds out for Clem to pilfer.

'True love. Soulmates, all that. Perhaps he writes her beautiful letters. Or has a rapier-sharp wit she both admires and envies…'

Ida scoffed. 'Hardly. Casterbury would have to have a soul to have a soulmate. Back to the plan –'

'Fine. Give me one more almond, first…'

Edith would be in position within the house itself. She'd serve drinks, smile, and keep Casterbury and his constable guests nicely tipsy and distracted so that Ida could get in, grab the main batch of Kaelinite from its hiding spot, and be out before anyone looked up from their drinks. Casterbury could keep his own home well-protected, just as long as no one else could. It wasn't much use to him. He wouldn't have anything The Rat Prince wanted after tonight, anyway.

It was a risky move, performing a job with a houseful of guests. But who would be wandering about in

Casterbury's bedrooms at a party? (Ida didn't want to know the answer to that.) Besides, her part was easy. Just get in and out, home before anyone knew she was gone.

'Ida, come with me.'

Ida was jolted back to the present as Lucinda whirled around in her seat, lunged across the bed and clasped Ida's hands in her own.

'Wh… but I..?'

'I won't know anyone there except for Odessa, and she'll be pestered all night by people wanting to know about her next expedition. I need someone with me at all times, in case… well, in case I need them. Unless you have a reason for wanting to stay at home, of course?'

Something strange came into Lucinda's expression, then; something steely, and slightly cunning. A chilly silence fell. Ida withdrew her hands, slowly.

'I… I only have my purple dress, ma'am.'

The strange expression was immediately gone. Lucinda was all smiles as she began raking through her jewellery collection.

'That's alright, darling! We can spruce it up a little bit. Let's see…what would go with purple?'

Ida's hand went to the pearl on a ribbon around her neck. It was only then that she realised she'd worn it most days since she fell from Clem's roof. Lucinda noticed it at approximately the same time. And apparently, because Ida had her own jewellery to wear, this somehow meant that Lucinda was allowed to put rouge on her instead. Joy. Ida didn't see the point, personally. She had perfectly decent blood vessels in her cheeks; why paint on more?

As Lucinda fussed with her furs and peeked out the window for the Horseless Casterbury had sent for them, Ida quickly crept back up to her room, grabbed her goggles, and slid them into the sewn-in pocket of her dress. Mam, she prayed as she hurried back downstairs, if you're there, please watch over me tonight. I think I'll need it.

Around an hour later, Lucinda and Ida disembarked from the Horseless. Somewhere along the way, it had begun to rain. Lucinda swept up the garden path, lit up in shades of cool blue by bio-luminescence. As Ida closed the carriage behind her, she felt a tap on her shoulder.

'Y'alright?' Clem asked, leaning against the door of the Horseless. Ida grabbed him by the lapel and dragged him into the road, round to the other side of the carriage.

'What are you doing here?' she hissed.

'I could ask you the same,' Clem said, looking her up and down. 'Can't remember the last time I saw The Rat Prince in a dress, although it would make the Loxport skyline more appealing…'

'Shut. Up.'

Ida shook him. Clem shoved her hands free and straightened his coat.

'I just wanted to be around. In case I was needed, you know?'

'Ida? Ida, darling, where have you gone… ?'

Ida groaned. 'I have to go. My life won't be worth living if she doesn't get her entrance.'

'Of course,' Clem said, rolling his eyes. 'just…'

He reached out and squeezed her hand.

'Be careful, please?'

He looked so pathetically, sweetly earnest. The swagger and the bravado of the Clem she had met at the exhibition wasn't gone, would never be gone. But it was hidden, tucked away for just a moment.

Ida winked at Clem; it was probably the first time she'd winked at anyone. He laughed. Their fingers lingered against each other's palms, just for a second. And then he was gone. Ida trotted to her mistress' side.

'Sorry, ma'am. I –'

'Let's just go inside,' Lucinda said, pushing the door open.

It was like standing in the middle of a belltower. In the corridor and drawing room beyond, guests who had arrived on time clapped their hands to their ears and yelped in pain. The Sentinel in action, Ida suspected.

Devon leapt to the rescue, dressed to the nines, or so he thought, in a burnished copper waistcoat and tie. He looked like a stove. His eyes looked red and puffy, as if he had not slept that night, and there was a certain hyperactive energy to him. He slammed a switch on the hallway wall, and the noise mercifully came to an end. After shooting the newcomer some disdainful looks, the guests went back to their mingling.

'Ladies, ladies,' Casterbury boomed, amicably welcoming them in. 'Do come in. No unexpected guests here, what? You must knock and wait. Or know the password, ha! You look wonderous, Lucinda, as always. Do come in, come along! One of the girls will take your coat.' When no such girl appeared, Ida ended up cradling Lucinda's furs. Her mistress smiled stiffly and accepted Casterbury's embrace, only to dance away as a familiar face emerged from the crowd.

'Odessa! Odessa, darling! It's so wonderful to see you, you look stunning!'

Even Ida had to admit, Odessa Malko was impossible to ignore. Possibly because she was the only woman wearing trousers. And not just any trousers; they were such a dark shade of blue they looked nearly black, with silver pinstripes that matched the buttons on her immaculately fitted waistcoat, on which she wore only a pocket watch. Was everyone in Loxport on a mission to educate Devon Casterbury on the elegance of colour choices?

Odessa welcomed Lucinda's hug with an affectionate squeeze. She had the same upper-class accent as the rest of Lucinda's ilk, but it was smooth, almost deep, and utterly sophisticated.

'Hello, Luci. How're you keeping?'

Lucinda flashed a grimace at her friend before cooing over her outfit instead of answering the question, and the two disappeared to find the bar. His beloved presently occupied, Casterbury wandered off in search of someone new to talk at. Ida fussed for an unoccupied peg on Casterbury's coat stand for a moment, before draping the fur over someone else's coat and hoping for the best. Wasn't she supposed to be playing chaperone?

Devon Casterbury's home was a study in useless opulence. The chandeliers were a mix of silver clockwork and crystal, sending rainbows around the room from the gaslit lamps affixed to the walls. The dining room was spotless, a long mahogany table boasting fruits and cheeses and many, many bottles of alcohol. Paintings and sculptures lined every wall, and it was only after a moment or two of looking that Ida realised Casterbury had hired the dancing automaton from the exhibition. As Ida scanned the crowd for Lucinda, a voice sliced through the hubbub around her.

'Aye, good man. We'll hafta have that pint sometime soon, iron out all the details.'

Something in Ida snapped to attention.

'I much prefer something a little... ahem, better aged, my friend. Let me tell you about this wonderful opium den I found on Gold Shawl Lane.'

Lounging in a high-backed chair as if he owned the place, glass of brandy in hand, was a man of about forty, chatting with Daniel, Lucinda's nephew. They were a study in different types of confidence; Daniel dressed to the nines in a dandelion-yellow suit jacket and a smirk. His top hat was trimmed in yellow silk and a tiny mechanical canary – probably his sister's work, Ida supposed – perched on his lapel. The other man wore no trimmings or smirks. His simple, dark grey suit stood out amongst the frippery and the finery around him, and yet he looked more like a king holding court than an outsider. How this man was the father of the nervous, witless Reggie, Ida would never understand. Terry Powell's wife must coddle their son beyond belief.

But of course, Ida thought, her jaw clenched so tight she thought the tendons might snap like piano wire. Of course, he's here too. At this rate, Nan's going to stroll through the door next and tell Casterbury his knick-knacks aren't up to standard.

Terry Powell was known for taking every opportunity he could lay his quick, deft fingers upon; news of Casterbury's new trinkets had already made its way to the unseemlier parts of Loxport, apparently. Perhaps he was here to get the jump on the constables, to see what they had in store and put plans into place so he and his associates could combat it, or at least survive it. Or perhaps he was simply sitting in a Lord's house to see how long he could get away with it. Ida could appreciate that, at least. But how had he managed to scrounge up an invite?

Someone tugged on her sleeve, yanking her attention away just as Daniel shook Powell's hand and leaned in close to whisper something, his mocking eyes sliding around the room.

'What are you doing here?'

It was Edith. Her hair was already working its way out from under her cap, and she was pink in the face.

'You,' she hissed, 'are meant to be outside! And are you wearing rouge? It looks weird!'

'I know that,' Ida hissed back. 'I made the plan, didn't I? Lucinda ordered me to come with her tonight.'

'What?'

'I know. And there wasn't much I could say, was there?'

'No, I suppose not.'

Edith took the brief second of stillness to whip her cap off her head and try in vain to tidy up her hair.

'So, what? We failed, try again another time? I suppose the information is still valid.'

'Oh no,' Ida huffed under her breath, 'I'm still going ahead. The Rat Prince loves a challenge. Besides, I have you here, don't I? My right-hand woman.'

Edith rolled her eyes and nudged her friend.   'Of course, you have me, you fool–'

'Excuse me?'

Edith and Ida looked up to see Odessa Malko towering over them. The corner of her mouth twitched up into a polite smile.

'Are you a serving girl tonight?' she asked Edith.

'Ar… ahm… um, I,' Edith replied.

'Could I have a drink for myself and my friend? Casterbury said there was a flagon of boysenberry liqueur stashed away somewhere, if I could track down a girl to get it for me.'

Malko tilted her head, and her bright blue eyes sparkled with some secret joke she wasn't sharing. 'If you don't mind, that is.'

'Aha… I… can… yes,' Edith continued. 'A drink! Sorry, that was…loud. I will get that. For you. I'll come back. Stay right here. Or don't. I'll find you. Thank you.'

Ida watched her friend, he right-hand woman, her best chance at some kind of cover tonight scurry off without saying goodbye, her cheeks burning so hot she was probably a fire hazard. She tripped over her shoes as she went.

This is going to be a disaster.

Chapter Thirty-One

———

Ida alternated between trailing behind Lucinda as she flitted from one conversation to another, dodging her way through walls of smart suits, and trying not to stand on any of the beautiful dresses that trailed the floor. All the while trying to map out Casterbury's home in her head. Forget about Powell. Forget about Daniel, forget about Edith and her ridiculous crush. If the dining room is below the master bedroom, then the back bedroom should be –

'Good evening, Ms. Belmonte.'

'Oh, Detective Oaken!'

And suddenly, right in front of her, was the rising star of the Loxport constabulary. He was tall, with the ramrod straight back of a man whose identity revolved around being respected by others. His moustache was thick and immaculate, and his eyes were the same slate grey as his cravat. He looked as if someone had grown him in a laboratory to be the ideal constable. Other, more common thieves of Loxport would be intimidated. But The Rat Prince, in disguise, merely curtsied, eyes open, mind sharp.

Detective Oakden nodded curtly at Lucinda.

'Your fiancé is going to make a great difference in this city, Ms. Belmonte. Or would you prefer Lady Casterbury?'

Lucinda's face went white.

'Well,' she stammered, covering her face with her fan, 'We aren't... that is to say, we haven't... officially...'

'Ma'am,' Ida said softly, touching her mistress' arm, 'your palpitations. I think we should find a quiet   corner to take your medication. Perhaps out in the fresh air?'

It took Lucinda a second to get the ruse, but once she did, she leaned on Ida for support and swooned. A little too much, but whatever.

'Yes, you are right, Ida; the heat, and the noise... come, let us sit outside for a moment, lovely to meet you at last, Detective, goodbye for now.'

'Er, goodbye, ma'am.' Devon Casterbury's garden was a lush, overpopulated affair. Everywhere you looked there were flowers, and trees dripping   blossom, and statues of Greek Goddesses. But it was quiet, lacking alcohol and music, and dark, the further back you walked. Lucinda went to sit directly on the grass, until Ida stopped her.

'Ma'am, perhaps a seat? There's a bench here, come along.'

She guided Lucinda to a bench as if she were a terrified puppy, and perched herself on the metal arm.

'Ida,' Lucinda whined, 'That was mortifying. To be informed of my own engagement by some plebian, as if that were his place! Ruined, all ruined...'

'I would wonder,' Ida said, treading lightly, 'if you

didn't know this was coming, ma'am.'

Lucinda stopped her whimpering and stared blankly ahead of her. Something rustled in the trees; a bird hopped in front of them, cheeky as you please, his oily black head cocked to one side, hoping to be given something tasty from them.

'I wonder about things, too,' she said, swishing her skirts in a vain attempt to scare the magpie off, 'I sometimes wonder why my dear Jonathan left me with such a clever maid. I'm not very clever myself, you know.'

Ida huffed a small laugh as the bird hopped forward again, almost like it was challenging Lucinda to a fight.

'I knew the house by then, and your routines. I'm quiet, and discreet. I fit well into your schedule. And I come to exhibitions with you without much   complaining.'

This was meant as a joke. Lucinda didn't laugh.

'Yes,' she said, after a pause. 'You are a good fit, for many reasons.'

Ida didn't know what to say to that, so she looked up at the stars. It was a nice, clear night; if she were on a roof, she could see the entire city on a night like this, and far off into the sea beyond. You could see the constellations: Callisto, Medusa, Orpheus. Then, her vision tilted a little more, and she was looking over her shoulder and up at the house. There it was: the large window with the red curtains. The Kaelinite was in there.

'What are you looking at?' Lucinda asked. Ida started.

'…the stars?'

Lucinda looked at Ida long and hard. In her stomach,

Ida felt a similar sensation to the one she had felt as she fell from Clem's roof. As if the world was swept out from underneath her unexpectedly.

'Lucinda? Lucinda, darling – come in from the cold, it's time for a toast!'

Casterbury. Both Ida and Lucinda winced, and then stood. The magpie took stock of the situation, realised there was no food to be had, and left, his wings flashing black and green in the candlelight. Casterbury had gathered everyone together in the dining room. The crowd felt like a thick blanket around Ida as they moved through it, and into the tiny circle where the man of the hour stood.

'Everyone,' he called, banging a spoon against a crystal wine flute, 'I would like to say a few words, if you please.'

'When don't you, Devon?' Parker bellowed from the back, his voice once again rich with wine. Casterbury bowed. He really was insufferable. Ida had no idea how she was going to cope with this for the rest of her career. The rest of her life.

'Yes, well. We are gathered here tonight to celebrate the official beginning of The Sentinel's line of duty in our fair city, of course. This is a triumph for the constabulary, for the inventors and thinkers who can piggy-back on this success to create their own security patents; and, of course, for Casterbury Emporiums, who will be stocking Sentinels for general purchase by Christmas.'

He actually held for applause. A light drizzle of clapping sprinkled through the crowd. They knew what they were really waiting for and wanted him to get on with it.

'But professional success is one thing,' he said, hand to heart. 'Personal happiness is also vital for a man to be fulfilled, healthy and wise. I have only known this wonderful woman for a short time in the grand scheme of my life, and yet I know that she is the only woman that is capable, level-headed, and savvy enough to stand at the helm of Casterbury Emporiums at my side. Lucinda Belmonte –'

Devon got down on one knee, fussed with his waistcoat a moment, then produced a ring box. Inside was an opulent pink diamond, flanked by tiny rubies, in a flamboyant Princess Cut. Clearly not some of Clem's work.

'– will you do me the honour, the pleasure and the privilege, of becoming my wife?'

The room held its breath. Some were already raising their own glasses up into a toast, ready to drink. Others were inching towards the couple, desperate to be the first to congratulate them. Across the room, Odessa Malko looked slightly sick. Lucinda's face, however, was blank. For a long moment. Then she tossed her curls, focused her eyes, stepped forward and gave her answer.

'No.'

The room erupted into chaos.

Chapter Thirty-Two

―――――

The noise, Ida suspected, was akin to something you would hear on a particularly rowdy day at the zoo. Men shouted, women implored, people of all genders pushed and pulled and tried to be both the first to hear Lucinda's reasons for turning the proposal down, and to get as far away from the entire situation as possible. Casterbury turned a sickly green colour and froze in place. Ida saw Terry Powell slip out the door, his top hat snatched from the mechanical hat spinner and a look of distaste curdling on his face.

Betrothal theatrics were clearly not to his taste. And all the while, the dancing automaton pirouetted on, her eyes far away and dreamy, her expression still fixed in a gentle smile. Ida was lost in a sea of hands and frills and voices, tossed and turned around and pushed further away from her mistress. She slipped through, diverting attention and turning the crowd so she could at least have some space to breathe. Between the bodies, she saw Edith being hustled away by her superior – she assumed it was Casterbury's own Cook – holding a huge and incredibly expensive-looking bottle of champagne. A wind-up corkscrew carved in the likeness of a heart was already embedded in the cork, its key primed for turning. The servants will be getting nicely drunk tonight, at least.

Lucinda was surrounded by a flock of dresses, all spinning and talking and crying at once. Odessa Malko was trying to extract her from the swarm, by force if necessary, icy with fury. Lucinda herself simply looked tired. Her gaze snagged on Ida's, and she widened her eyes in a meaningful way. Ida tried to reach her. Lucinda widened her eyes more, shaking her head. Ida tilted her head, confused. Lucinda mouthed 'GO'.

What? What is happening? Does Lucinda…

No time.

Ida backed up as slowly as she dared, until the backs of her feet hit Casterbury's curving marble staircase. Then she bolted up them.

In a stark change of pace, the upstairs floors were quiet and cool, much as they had been the last time Ida was here. She resisted the temptation to take off her shoes and creep silently along the plush carpet; rather, she closed her eyes for a fraction of a second to get her bearings. I'm over the dining room, so this is the master bedroom, and this must be…

Wrong. Ida found herself in a porcelain white bathroom, the clawfoot tub in the middle gleaming white as a tooth, its gold feet like fillings. Ida had the dim realisation she'd never had a bath, just a wash, before closing the door.

So where is it? Think, Rat Prince, think…

A linen closet, filled with those gaudy waistcoats. She was rushing, not thinking. Beneath her, Odessa Malko was calling for order, while the gents had congregated in another corner and were braying their disapproval like members of parliament. Casterbury's voice, could not be heard, for once.

I haven't got time for this! Right. This one…

Finally; success. The room itself was all reds and dark burgundies. The bed was wide and soft-looking, the covers made of silk. The faint scent of jasmine floated over Ida. It was definitely a different bedroom to the one Ida had used to enter the building when she was last here. This one must have been where Casterbury entertained his… Oh, God.

After Ida gave herself a mental image she would have to boil out of her brain later, she braced herself, took a deep breath, went to step into the room and stopped. There, mounted on the wall, was a rectangular shape, about the size of a shoebox, casting the smallest hint of green light over the floor. Of course, he'd set up a Sentinel in here, too. Ida grinned. Time to see what this thing was made of. The biggest, riskiest job of her career. And time was not on her side.

It felt like Christmas.

Slowly, she crouched onto the floor, and fished her goggles from her pocket. As she fitted them over her eyes and fixed the settings so she could see the faintest outline of the Sentinel's light through their lenses – not an easy task, with green lenses, but not impossible – she let a happy shudder run down her back. At least this felt right.

From what Clem said, the light was the sensitive area

for the Sentinel. The one at the front door   covered the
threshold; this one looked like it covered a very specific
part of the room; from the left-hand wall to the foot of
the bed, in a tight rectangle. So, their range is small, Ida
supposed. For now.

Ida crawled on her stomach (her foot getting
dangerously tangled in her skirts) until she was just
beside the end of the Sentinel's range. Underneath it
was a standard safe, no extra locks or combinations to
puzzle through. Casterbury must have really had faith
in his new toy. The beam went down, onto the floor,
and out, into the air in front of and above the safe. Like
Edith said, the front of the Sentinel was parchment,
which let the light shine through.

Alright, Ida thought. Just need to find a way to disable
the light –

Suddenly, a puff of warm steam tousled the top of
her head. The small beam that jutted out of the wall
juddered ever-so-slightly, and then began to move. It
pivoted towards her, and Ida scrambled further into
the darkness of the bedroom, away from the beam of
light. It reached the end of its trajectory, the light almost
touching the threshold, then stopped. A pause, another
tiny shudder, and the mechanism swept the Sentinel
back across the bedroom floor, right to the far window.
In about twenty seconds, the Sentinel had tripled the
width of its scope.

Fantastic.

Ida crouched beside the bed and watched the green

bar of light cross the floor again as she thought. The Kaelinite must be powering both the alarm system and the movement. Casterbury would be rubbing his hands together. They were adapting the thing even before it was available to buy, and whichever inventors and mechanics he had freelanced to make the damned thing had found a way to stop all the pent-up energy from blowing up in their faces. Ida stopped. Images from the night she had stolen the Kaelinite from the Schuyler flashed before her eyes. The sudden burst of bright light. And the foam; the foam that had seeped out from the stone as she pressed it into her chest, begging not to be seen from below. If the Kaelinite overheated, it gave off a foam to cool itself down. That's why she hadn't been burned at the Schuyler. Her tunic had been soaked with cold, wet foam…

She needed to get up close to the mechanism.

As the Sentinel began its journey away from the door, Ida grabbed a footstool and wedged it next to the side panel of the safe. She stood upon it – not high enough – and leapt away back to her hiding spot as the green beam returned. Next time, she had a huge, ornate hardback book in hand. The spine had barely even been cracked. A great bibliophile, that Casterbury. Standing on her tiptoes, her fingers just brushed against the screws that embedded the Sentinel to the wall. She needed one more thing to stand on, and she could use her lockpick hook to loosen the screws –

'Is anyone up here?'

The clipped voice of Detective Oakden rang out

from the end of the hallway. Ida dove away from her precarious tower, back towards the bed. There was someone with him. Not Casterbury, but another male voice she didn't recognise.

'Sir,' the second voice said, 'I think we're of better use downstairs. That crowd is beginning to sour.'

'And we shall go back down,' Oakden snapped. 'Once I have made sure everything is secure up here. I thought I saw someone…'

If he turned the bedroom's gas lamp on, he would see her. Without thinking, Ida slid under the covers of the bed. The sheets were cool against her skin.

'Hello?' Oakden called out again, his footsteps louder now, even on the plush carpet.

Then Ida Finn, The Rat Prince, did something she had never done before in her nineteen years on this earth.

She giggled.

Chapter Thirty-Three

———

'Hello?' Oakden asked again. He rapped sharply on the door of the bedroom, his fellow constable lingering on his heels.

Ida giggled again, picturing Lucinda at her bubbliest in every hitch of her voice. Think brainless, Ida. Think posh and rich and without a care in the world…

'Is someone –'

'Erm, Sir?' the second voice said, hesitant and embarrassed. 'I… I don't think that's a good idea.'

Ida rustled the sheets above her head with her hands, shushing herself in a lower, raspier voice – her Rat Prince voice, if The Rat Prince ever got sloshed out of his mind on expensive wine and seduced a duchess. Which he hadn't.

'Shush, darling, I haven't ravished you adequately yet…'

Was this right? Was this what amorous people did?

'Oh. Erm. Ahem…' Detective Oakden cleared his throat, trying to sound in charge of the situation. 'Detective Oakden, of the Loxport constabulary. Is everything… alright?'

'Yes, yes, constable! All is well in here.'

Ida tittered, her cheeks crimson with frustration and humiliation, her hand clamped against her tightly-closed eyes. Go away, please just go away.

'Sir, can we please go?' the constable pleaded with his boss.

Another clearing of the throat.

'Please come back down to the dining room, as soon as you're… dressed.' Oakden finished his sentence weakly. 'Or I'll have you escorted from the building.'

'Just kill me now,' the other constable whimpered.

'Officer Caplin!'

'Sorry, sir.'

'Yes, yes, we'll be right along.' Lucinda-Ida said, listening for two sets of shoes briskly walking back along the landing and downstairs. When there was quiet (or as much quiet as she could find, given that someone downstairs had decided to sing, off-tune, to lighten the spirits), she slid out from under the covers, and grabbed another hardback from the shelves. This time, as the green light moved away from her, she had just enough height to reach her goal. She'd have to act quickly, now, before someone came looking for an amorous, entirely imagined couple.

A few quick twists of her lockpick hook, and the screw was loosened. Back to the hiding spot, until it was safe to move her tower over and do the same on the other side. Then back one more time, to wait.

Each judder of the Sentinel hitting its destination grew more and more pronounced. Each time it came to a stop, the beam shuddered across the floor. The light brightened, but dark, wet patches began to bloom on the parchment as well. Bubbles began to form at the corners. After a few minutes, the light behind the canvas began to flicker and dim. The movements and the shuddering became slower and slower, and then –

Darkness. It had worked.

Ida crept, inch by inch, towards the safe. Globs of pale green foam were seeping through the parchment, dripping in viscous bubbles onto the carpet. Being careful not to leave any footprints in the damper patches, Ida began working on cracking the safe.

Despite everything, she felt her mind slip into that relaxed, happy state – the same feeling she always had when lockpicking. She knew this part. Foaming gemstones with magic energy properties were outside her general wheelhouse. This, she could do.

Trying to block out the racket from downstairs, Ida pressed her ear to the safe and began, oh so slowly – far too slowly for her liking – to feel out the combination, listening for the different noises of the lock to tell her their secrets.

Deep inside the safe, the first wheel clicked into place. One down.

Someone downstairs was asking where Lucinda was. No noise on the landing yet, though. Hopefully she was sitting in the garden with one of those bottles of wine, drowning whatever emotions she was feeling. Or she'd gone home and forgotten about her maid.

Click. Another wheel in place.

Now she just had to find the last one. There! No, that wasn't right… God, this safe is rusty as hell… concentrate, girl…

This was taking too long. Someone could come up those

stairs any second. A partygoer, the constables, Casterbury –

There. The most satisfying sound in the world; the final clunk of the arm inside the safe's mechanism falling into place. Ida opened the safe as slowly as she dared and there, on top of a white handkerchief, was the main source of Kaelinite. Ida smoothly slipped it into the pocket of her dress, stood up, and closed the safe. Relief washed over her, hot and cold at the same time. Now, she just needed to get out. Past a group of drunk elites and suspicious constables, who would all be watching for any comings and goings in case there was more excitement to be had tonight.

Her gaze slid to the window.

It was far harder to drop from a window ledge in skirts than it was in trousers. As Ida clambered onto the sill, rain whipped at her face. It must have started pouring sometime after Lucinda refused Casterbury's proposal. Fitting.

Gripping the top of the window frame as she stood, Ida gauged her surroundings. The ground below her was blurry through the rain, which stuck to her goggles in thick smears, making it harder to see. Her dress clung to her thighs within seconds. The drainpipe was not far from the window, just over an arm's breadth away. She could reach that. She'd jumped longer distances half-asleep. Just never while there was what sounded like a riot going on inside the building. She lunged for the drainpipe. For a heart-stopping second, she thought she had it. Then her feet snagged on the edges of her skirt. The painted metal of the drainpipe slid over her fingertips, and then she was falling, with nothing to catch her. Her goggles – and her mam – were no help to her now.

Pain spiked up her legs and arms in waves as she landed on her knees in the mercifully soft earth of a well-loved flower bed. Thank goodness for gardeners who were over-zealous with their peat soil. She tumbled forward, gently faceplanting into the mud. She'd definitely opened up the gash in her leg again, she could feel the blood trickling down her calf. The gem was glowing in her pocket from the shock of the fall, just enough so the material of her pocket couldn't hide it. A mix of foam, rainwater and mud coated her hip. Ida crouched amongst the plants and bushes, praying for it to calm down inside. She could hear male voices just at the door to the garden, looking out at the rain.

'Ida? Ida!'

Oh, no. Of course.

Clem ran from a tree near the back of the property. He was soaked through – how long had he been there?

'Can you stand up? Can you walk?' he whispered, trying to pull Ida to her feet. He was trampling all over Casterbury's flowerbeds. It would be funny if she hadn't just fallen out of a window.

'I said I'd be here if you needed me, didn't I?' Clem was saying as he inspected the cuts on her legs. He was so gentle that Ida's chest hurt. Or maybe that was from the fall, too.

'Clem, you need to go,' Ida hissed. 'I'm fine, but you'll give us away!'

'I'm not going to leave you here,' he said, his hand around her arm. Ida fished the still-glowing Kaelinite from her pocket. The noise from inside the party was bearing down on her, and she swore she could hear the blood rushing in her veins. She suddenly realised that if Clem got caught in this garden and arrested for trespassing, she would never forgive herself.

'Take it,' she said, pushing the Kaelinite against Clem's chest. 'Take it and go.'

'I'm not leaving you bleeding in a garden, mate.' Clem tried to look intimidating. Instead, he simply knotted his eyebrows together. 'Ida –'

'If I get arrested, I am not taking you down with me!' Ida spat, shoving Clem away from her. 'Now go, or we'll both get caught anyway.'

Clem glared at her. Ida held his gaze. Finally, he backed away, still holding the gem near his heart. Then, mercifully, he turned and ran. As he disappeared back into the darkness of the far end of the garden, Ida whipped her now-filthy goggles into her pocket and brushed off the leaves and dirt from her dress as best she could in the dark and stumbled onto the lawn, trying to see Edith inside the house. She could give her a cover story – she fell in the garden, perhaps, or had some kind of fainting spell, and needed to find Ms. Belmonte right away.

'What are you doing out here?'

The voice of the young Officer who had been at the bedroom doorway made Ida spin. He looked about Reggie Powell's age and didn't even have the traditional constable's moustache.

'What happened?'

'I… fell,' Ida stammered, gesturing to the flowerbed. 'The noise, it was all too much for me. I think I should go home; I need to find my mistress,'

The young officer extended a hand to her. 'Alright, just this way, miss–'

'Hang on a second, Officer Caplin.'

Detective Oakden strode out from the house, a cigarette dangling from his lips. He didn't seem to care much that it wouldn't stay lit for long in this weather.

'Aren't you Lucinda Belmonte's maid?'

Ida nodded, thinking it best to keep her mouth shut.

'She's been through a lot tonight.' Oakden tossed the now damp cigarette into the dark. 'Why aren't you with her? I'm sure she could use her staff at her side while she goes through…whatever's going on with her tonight. What are you doing out here that's more important than your job?'

Two thoughts sped through Ida's brain. Run and – impossibly, stupidly – fight. To the end. Don't let them take you alive. She'd never longed for her knife more.

'You're injured, too. More than from just tripping over, I'd wager.'

'Has someone inside the party hurt you, Miss? Someone out here?'

'I think you need to come with us regardless,' Oakden said, stepping towards her. He didn't have the expression of a man who thought he was dealing with a victim.

Ida gritted her teeth and said nothing. If they touch me, I'll bite them so hard the scars will never leave them, so deeply that they won't be able to look at their own flesh without thinking of how The Rat Prince died fighting, died screaming – died a girl, died a maid, under their nose until the very end.

If I get through this, I'm never talking to Nan again.

'Ida, darling! There you are!'

Ida was suddenly enveloped in ruffles. Lucinda pressed her damp cheek against Ida's and stifled a sob.

'I know I said before that I wanted to stay and talk to Devon, but tonight is simply irretrievable! I want to go home right now, and I shall not be using his hideous Brightwind carriage to do it! Oh, and look – you've slipped! I keep telling you, dear; that style of dress is far too long for someone of your height. Let's walk home, Ida dear. I think the fresh spring air will calm my nerves. Thank you, Officers, for looking after her, she's the only light in my life, my dearest companion. Goodnight! Goodnight!'

And, just like that, Lucinda glided out of her own engagement party, her ring finger still bare and her head held high. And Ida Finn, The Rat Prince, trailed along behind her out into the dark, filthy and shaken. The night air turned the sweat on her brow to ice water, until Innovation Court was nothing more than an unpleasant memory.

Chapter Thirty-Four

———

Clem weighed the green gem in his hand, whistling gently.

'So… Kaelinite, huh?' he said, almost to himself. 'To think: Clem Magnesan holds in his hands the most powerful technological asset in Loxport.'

He looked up at Ida and Edith, grinning. 'Who wants a new pair of green earrings?'

Edith flung out her leg and kicked him in the shin.

'You really are an idiot.'

Ida nodded emphatically. She had too many sugared almonds in her mouth to reply. Edith had persuaded her to pop to Mimi's with her before they came to Clem's ('to stretch your legs, Ida, you don't want to get stiff…'). Turns out, they sold sugared almonds that were even nicer than the ones at Potter's Street market. She and Edith had gone halves on the biggest bag they sold – a concoction of half almonds and half caramel cogs that would baffle the most unhinged scientist in the city – and their hands kept dipping idly into the bag as they sat on Clem's chaise. Ida still mostly picked out the almonds though.

The ill-fated party was the talk of Loxport. All signs pointed to The Rat Prince pulling off another one of his daring escapades. There was even a rumour that he had seduced someone at the party – a lady of high standing! – to gain access to the bedroom where the only source of power for Devon Casterbury's newest project was hidden. Perhaps there had been a whole gang of criminals right under their noses. There were multiple footprints in the garden, just under the window.

And, of course, Devon Casterbury had been rejected in front of most of Loxport. That was interesting, too. Lucinda had been plagued with 'well-wishers' wanting to be the first to hear the gossip, and Ida had been kept very busy telling most of the city that Ms. Belmonte was not accepting visitors at the moment, thank you so very much.

'You're not having nightmares or anything, you said?' Ida asked, washing the sugar out her mouth with a swallow of tea. 'You've had the Kaelinite for a few days, now.'

'Not at all! I've come up with a solution, you see,' Clem said breezily, waving a hand in her direction. 'I'm working myself to the bone at my smithy, so at night I just collapse into an exhausted, dreamless slumber every night. Working like a charm so far,   until I can come up with something better. Don't fret, dear friends, don't fret.'

'Hm.' Ida grunted, unconvinced.

'So,' Edith said, hopping up from the chaise in Clem's smithy, 'are we all off to The Boathouse for celebratory tea? Ida's treat, remember?'

Edith had taken it upon herself to spend Ida's money for her; in a purely supportive way, of course. Until they could find some way of Ida living on her own and putting the money towards her bills. 'That is,' Clem had laughed, 'if Lucinda will let you.'

Ida knew that would never happen. Her role at the Belmonte house was to be a constant companion, as well as a housekeeper. The only way she could move out was if she moved on. And she wasn't sure about that quite yet.

After all, where would she find such a good cover?

'Yeah,' Clem said, flipping his shop sign from 'open' to 'closed'. 'Sounds great, Edie. Can I have a word with Ida first, though? I've got a few ideas I want to put to her.'

'Oh, that is fine, Clem! Absolutely fine!'

Edith thought she was being subtle when she poked Clem in the side and giggled. She wasn't. 'I shall be outside, around the corner, out of sight, waiting for whenever you two are done with your conversation about... ideas.'

'Thanks, Edie,' Clem deadpanned, shutting the door in her face. Ida laughed.

'She's my best friend,' she said, powering through the awkwardness of the new phrase on her tongue, 'but I don't understand her.'

'She's great.' Clem said. 'Nice to have a fellow ginger around. Solidarity, y'know? Has she gotten over her little incident at the party?'

'With The Scientist? She's getting there, in time. She only talked about it for half an hour on the way here.'

Ida tucked her legs underneath her and stretched. Clem plopped himself down on the chaise next to Ida.

He stifled a yawn, and Ida noticed that his eyes were red-rimmed.

'Tired?' she asked.

'Yeah,' Clem said through another yawn. 'Been working too hard, I suppose. So…'

'So?'

'I had a few ideas,' Clem blurted out. 'About what to do with the Kaelinite.'

'I thought you wanted to use it for yourself?' Ida asked. Clem shrugged, shifty all of a sudden.

'I've been thinking: we can't very well sell it on right away, can we? Everyone in Loxport will be looking for it – the Night Market, the constables, Casterbury… so what I was thinking was I could keep wheedling my way into the good graces of people like your Ms. Belmonte, get myself a real patron and then, when I know how to control it, I can say 'oh look, I just happened to have all these plans and a brand new seam of Kaelinite that fell out of a dirigible."

'That sounds like a lot of work.'

'And time,' Clem agreed. 'So, in the interim I thought, why not give The Rat Prince a little upgrade? Keep him one step ahead, at least for a while?'

'Will that be alright?' Ida asked. 'The nightmares… I can't have them come back.'

'Don't you worry about that, I'm working on it. Secret and cunning plans, I'll have it cracked by the time you can turn around three times. Here, look.'

 He produced some scrolls of paper from his back

pocket, and handed them to Ida like the hilt of a sword.

'The one I'm really excited about is for the goggles. I mean,' he scratched the back of his head as he spoke, looking away, 'if I'm allowed to touch them. I know they're important to you.'

'They are. They were my mam's.'

'Ah. Well, forget that one,' Clem said, making to grab the scroll from her. 'Look at the next one. I was thinking about some sort of powered drill, quiet enough to use in houses, to break safes faster and –'

'No, hang on.' Ida held the blueprints tightly in her hand. 'I've been thinking about them too. I don't think my mam would want me to sacrifice my safety for the sake of sentimental value. They're pretty old now, you know? Old-fashioned, too. I'll look at it over tea, alright? No promises. But if you're careful –'

'Ida,' Clem clamped his hand to his chest, 'I would handle them as carefully as if they were the Princess Victoria's own diamonds. As if they were the most delicate of crystals, the most valuable of treasures from the darkest –'

'Do you ever shut up?' Ida yelled, thwacking him with a cushion. Clem jumped up from the chaise, out of her way, and Ida flopped over, resting her head on the arm of the chaise, looking up at Clem.

'What have I got to do to make your brain stop going a mile a minute?'

She grinned at him, triumphant that she had claimed the entire space as her own. Clem's expression went strange, then soft. He knelt down so his nose was almost touching Ida's. His eyes still bore straight into her own. She turned, so she could see him better. He smelled like fresh linen, clean, and warm.

'I have a few ideas.'

Ida felt something she'd never felt before; certainly not when Luca Black had tried to kiss her when she was nine. A strange, magnetic, inevitable feeling, as Clem leaned over her and his lips just barely brushed against hers. They were soft, and gentle. His fingers ran along her jawline and cupped her chin. Her eyes closed, for the briefest of blinks, and then...

'Wait,' she whispered.

Clem lurched back as if he'd been scorched.

'Sorry!' he cried, scuttling away from her across the smithy shop floor, his back colliding with the bench behind him. 'I just... I... thought that... oh, hell. Oh god.'

Ida sat up on the chaise, leaning on the arm so she could look at him. The afternoon at Lucinda's house, where he had tried to speak to her alone, suddenly made a little more sense.

'Clem –'

'Can we still be friends?' Clem babbled. 'Just... forget all about it, I was being stupid, I haven't been – maybe Edith has a friend she can set me up with. I could go back to courting gents for a spell, perhaps. Gents are easier. Or...'

'Clem!'

He froze. Ida slid off the chaise and sat beside him. He winced.

'Is it...?'

Clem gestured up and down his frame, before his thoughts got away from him and he was twirling his wrist in abstract circles in the air. He changed track with a slight cough. 'Have I done something wrong?'

'Never. Remember,' she said, her shoulder nudging his, 'a month ago I didn't even let myself have friends.'

'I know,' Clem sighed.

'It's still all so confusing to me. How much do I say, when do I say it, what do friends even do together, aside from tea?'

'And occasional heist planning, and punching each other, and thwarting of the constabulary, and –'

'And that. So...more than friends, with anyone...is still a way away for me. It's too much right now.'

'That makes sense,' Clem said with a sigh. 'I never intended to rush you, or pressure you.' He looked at her, and his hand slid into hers. 'I'm not going anywhere, Ida Finn. You are far too interesting for that. But if that means being your friend, instead of...whatever half-cooked idea I just had in my head... that's wonderful. We can just do crimes and have tea, ad infinitum.'

Ida felt warm inside. Happy. Accepted. It was unusual, and quite nice. In fact, ever since the night of the heist, she'd been sleeping well, feeling better, and generally back to her old self, more or less. The wonders of a job well done and of working as a team, she supposed.

'Oh, speaking of tea...'

Clem dug his elbow into Ida's, and pointed to the window. The coppery crown of Edith's head could be seen at the side of the smithy window as she pretended that she wasn't snooping. Ida groaned, and pulled herself up.

'We have to get her with that Scientist woman,' Clem said, offering a hand to Ida. 'It's the only way we'll have any sanity.'

An entire conversation happened between Edith and Clem in the space of a few blinks as they locked the smithy door behind them. Ida couldn't keep up, but she got the gist. Edith pouted in commiseration at Clem, before throwing her arms around both him and Ida.

'Right!' she chirped. 'The Boathouse! Tea! Sweets! Cats!'

'And,' Clem said, squeezing Edith tight, 'I have another idea to float past you, ladies. If a certain member of rodent royalty gets to have an exciting moniker, I think we all should have one, as well. We are all part of the criminal elite now, you know.'

'Ooh!' said Edith. 'Can I be The Vixen? 'cos of my hair, you know?'

She pushed her chest out in a way Ida supposed was meant to be sultry and pouted through a wall of curls. 'Oh, and Clem could be... hm. The Dragon? Because you work with fire?'

'As poetic and subtle as those names are,' Clem laughed, dancing in front of the two girls, walking backwards as he spoke. 'I was thinking of a group name. Watch out, wealthy and powerful citizens of Loxport: for they are always with you.' His voice dropped into a dark, sinister tone, like a man onstage at the theatre preparing you for a murder mystery play.

'Spying, infiltrating your safe little houses, your gentlemen's clubs. Their beady eyes will spot your treasure, swoop in, and have it whisked away before you can say 'stocks and bonds.' They are clever, they are cunning, and they are utterly, utterly wicked. Loxport; prepare yourself… for The Clockwork Magpies.'

He ended with a flourish; spinning around a lamppost, one arm flung wide, grinning toothily. Silence.

'I,' Ida said flatly, 'will never, ever call us that.'

Chapter Thirty-Five

———

Edith was adamant that they walked along the river. As they did, they passed the section of the bank where they had jettisoned their stolen boat. They shared a look behind Clem's back, and grinned.

They passed the opening to Tarnish Street. Ida hadn't been there today. Or for a while.

The trio spent a happy hour and a half in the Boathouse, being bothered by Dougie the cat and getting dizzy from the sheer amount of rose-pink buttercream on their slices of Princess Sponge Cake. The sun was streaming in the teahouse window, warming the crown of Ida's head. Edith was retelling the story of her embarrassing evening with regards to The Scientist to Clem, gesturing wildly and barely attempting to keep her voice down – much to the chagrin of the other customers and to the dismay of Beth, who could be spotted diving into a tray of honeycomb tiffin to lift her mood via sugar.

'…and then I got her the damned bottle of liqueur, and you know what she said?'

Clem swallowed a mouthful of tea.

'"Oh thank you, you angel?" Like she did last time you told me this story?'

Edith slammed down her fork and glared daggers at Clem.

'Yes,' she growled. 'What does that even mean?!'

'I think she was gasping for a drink, and the maid had wandered off to have palpitations in the back somewhere.'

'I just don't know what I'll do, Clem…'

Ida's stomach lurched. Guilt, deep and black, seared suddenly through her veins.

She'd lain in bed the night after the heist, thinking over what she'd thought as she stared down the constables. Mostly the part where she made a vow never to speak to her Nan again. What a strange thing to think about, as your entire life is about to fall apart.

Her fork must have chittered against her plate, because Edith had gently taken it away from her.

'Are you thinking about what we talked about on the way to Clem's?' she asked gently. Ida nodded.

'Remember,' Edith said, 'we decided she gets half the money she used to. Dropped off at the door. She won't starve. But she doesn't get to hoard what you give her like… like an ogre.'

'Do ogres hoard?' Clem pondered into the dregs of his cup.

'And she doesn't get to talk to you like that anymore.'

'But my mam wouldn't want –'

'Your mam wouldn't want you to be feel like this, either.' Edith brandished her teapot at Ida.

'You aren't going back in that house, Ida Finn. Because I say so. Got it?'

'Do you remember,' Clem said, leaning across the table,

'telling me once that one should not care about people who insist on being idiots?'

'…yes,' Ida admitted with a groan.

'Good. Don't worry,' Clem added, as he stood up to grab yet another slice of cake, squeezing Ida's shoulder as he passed, 'we'll keep you right.'

'I'm sure of that,' she said. There would be repercussions with Nan, she was sure of it. But they were a way off. And, right now, in this moment, that was enough.

Soon, the three of them were saying goodbye. Edith hugged Ida tightly as they turned onto Juniper Avenue, and then, with a big wave, she was gone. Ida hopped up the light grey stone steps at the front of the house.

As she opened the front door, the house was quiet. More than that: the silence was heavy, almost expectant.

'Ma'am?' Ida called as she gently closed the door behind her. 'It's just me. I'm back. I'll be upstairs in my bedroom if you –'

'Ida?'

'Yes, ma'am?'

'Can you come here, please?'

Ida made her way into the drawing room where her employer sat on a chaise lounge, examining the ruffles of her light pink petticoat.

'I met with Daniel and Eloise, a fortnight or so ago. I don't think I ever told you.'

'Oh?'

'I haven't seen them for a little while, and now that Eloise is much better, I wanted to take them both for tea. Do you remember that Eloise makes clockwork animals? She has since childhood, always fascinated with them. I remember that she used to make us little deer with watch springs inside their legs. She's a clever, wonderous child. Too clever, some may say. She'll never find a husband. Oh, will you please dust the mantel? Thank you, darling.'

Lucinda knew Ida was off the clock. She reached awkwardly towards the duster, her eyes fixed on Lucinda, head tilted quizzically.

'And so, because she has a love of nature and of machinery, when Daniel was last… 'away from home', shall we say… he stumbled across a gorgeous little piece on a market stall that he thought would make for inspiration for her, especially when she's been so ill. He told her to show me, and she did.'

The older woman held up a hand, and Ida paused, fingers brushing the duster.

'Now, I can be silly, sometimes, and a tad forgetful. But, as I studied her new toy, I thought it looked decidedly familiar. Go on, darling. Dust away, as I speak to you.'

There was a shape underneath the duster. Ida pinched the material between forefinger and thumb and lifted it away.

'We never stand on ceremony in this house, do we?'

Lying on the mantle, slightly scratched and dinged but still beautiful, was a butterfly brooch, set with rubies the size of her thumb.

Ida was running before the last words were out of Lucinda's mouth. Her heart, rabbit-like with panic, thrummed in her throat, her mind sickly green and tilted. Stupid mistake, trusting a bloody Powell – especially the bairn. What was she thinking?! She'd been in such a damn hurry to get rid of that damned blasted thing...

She needed to get out. More than that, she needed to be out the city before the constables could even knock on Lucinda's door.

The house she'd lived in for so long was suddenly a maze. Where could she run? Up the stairs, into Lucinda's quarters. The window bolted and padlocked. That was new. Further up still, into her quarters – if she could make it to the roof, she could... could...

Get tangled in her dress again and break her neck, most likely. Her Rat Prince garb was locked away in a trunk under her bed. She'd run out of time.

Her mother's goggles were in that trunk. She'd lost them for good.

'Ida. Get back here. Now.'

There was a steel in Lucinda's voice as she climbed the steps that Ida had never heard there before. She took a half-step towards her mistress, before realising what she was doing. Lucinda glided along the hallway towards her, the brooch in her hand, the delicate swish of her skirts the only sound. Ida swallowed hard.

'Give me ten minutes, Lucinda. Five, even – and I'll be gone. I'll leave your life, leave Loxport, and never come back. Just please, don't call for the constables.'

Lucinda smiled, and Ida's stomach dropped.

'I know what you did, Ida. I know you stole this

brooch from me. It was a gift from Lord Casterbury, and you took it. And it's not the only thing you've taken, is it? Perhaps not from me, but from others like me?'

Ida nodded, appalled at herself for doing so. She felt like an automaton, just obeying commands. Lucinda had never, ever spoken to her this way before. Lucinda contemplated her steadily, then, holding her arm out over the bannister, dropped the butterfly brooch down the stairs. Ida heard it tinkling as it hit step after step.

'Do you know what Jonathan used to call me?' Lucinda asked. Ida shook her head. 'Precious. He used to call me Precious. If I was getting myself worked up about something silly, like a forgotten invitation or what to wear to the opera, he'd take my hands, smile and say 'Now, Precious – aren't we being a little foolish?' And, usually, I was. Ida, I know I'm... hard work, sometimes. I let things run away with me. I feel things very strongly, sometimes. And when he died, I thought to myself 'Well, there you are, Lucinda. The only person who could tolerate your foolishness, the only one who loved it and could stop it in its tracks... and now he's gone.' And then Devon began to court me.'

Lucinda sat down on the top step of the staircase. She looked very much like a flower, Ida thought – or the buttercream from that Princess Sponge cake.

'I was so ready to be loved again, Ida. For someone to take my hands and smile at me again. Another chance to have a family. And, as he finally proposes to me, he calls me level-headed. Ida, I have never been level-headed even once in all my life! And, in that moment, I realised why I'd been so sad, why I had wanted you with me that evening, despite knowing by then that you had stolen from me. He was never right for me… and you've been watching over me for months, haven't you? That's why you took that awful brooch. To send me a message about Devon. I was so blind, and he was always a cad; so rude, and uncouth, and badly dressed – and you knew all along.'

And that brooch was worth ninety Athenas. Ida kept her back straight and her mouth shut and waited to see where this all was going. A move she instantly regretted, as Lucinda leapt to her feet, stormed along the hall, and pulled her into a tight, teary hug. Two hugs in one day – a new record for Ida Finn.

'I knew that whatever you were doing at the party must be justified. Because you are good, Ida. You simply must stay, darling. I'd be simply lost without you.'

After perhaps a moment longer than necessary, Ida extracted herself from Lucinda's embrace, holding her at arm's length.

'Ma'am… Lucinda. If I stay, I won't change, you know I am The Rat Prince before I am anything else, so if you take umbrage with that, call the constables now and I can try to outrun them…'

'…you're The Rat Prince?'

Lucinda blinked, and Ida's spine was a pillar of ice. 'I thought you were just a common thief.'

'Lucinda…'

'Oh, that is even better!' Lucinda said, tossing her blonde curls.

'…I'm sorry,' Ida said. 'I'm confused. Do I need to run, or not?'

'If I was willing to keep you if you were merely a scoundrel,' Lucinda laughed, 'why would a little thing like being a master criminal stop me from employing you? It's now your greatest asset!'

'What… do you mean…?'

Something in Lucinda's round, blue eyes turned steely. Ida was frightened.

'Do you have your next target in mind?'

Chapter Thirty-Six

———

God, it felt good to be The Rat Prince again.

Ida bounced from rooftop to rooftop like a squirrel. She let herself hang from drainpipes and swing from streetlamps, dart through the shadows like a ghost and hitch a ride, for a street or two, from a Horseless filled with drunken students. She drifted through the city, pickpocketing aimlessly, just for fun.

Things were strange now. Detective Oakden and his partner had knocked on the door exactly once, wanting to take information from everyone who was at the fateful party. Lucinda had offered them tea and done all the talking, as was expected, and Ida had nodded shyly and said things like 'that's right, ma'am' until the constables had gone away. But still, the force were humiliated, and now they were doubling their efforts to find The Rat Prince. Even tonight, Ida had had to dodge more looming shadows in tall hats than she ever had before – and that would be only the beginning. Detective Oakden did not seem like a man to take a little embarrassment lightly, let alone allowing the most wanted person in the city escape from a building he himself was in.

Devon Casterbury – even though he was no longer

bothering Lucinda with pleading letters and flowers and boxes of chocolates, would also be out for revenge. He couldn't punish Lucinda, not really, and so Ida was in the line of fire. That night at Innovation Court had been one of the most mortifying of his life; losing his assumed fiancée and his new business venture in one night. Stocks for Casterbury Emporiums had fallen; not enough to threaten bankruptcy, Lucinda informed her, but enough to sting. The Rat Prince had some powerful enemies, these days.

But then, she had her allies. Not all the elite was out for her blood. Even tonight, she was on her way to pilfer plans from Charles McConnell. Something about a manufactured brain, the most developed machine in the something something something. The only thing that mattered was the three hundred fifty Athenas waiting for her when the job was done. A nice little dent in her house fund.

Lucinda had taken to the role of Patron of Criminals scarily quickly. Once she knew everything about the – ugh – 'Clockwork Magpies' situation, she had proven to be excellent at dropping hints into conversations with her closest friends that there were certain someones who could help them with any little predicaments they had – she'd learned about it from a former acquaintance who must remain nameless. Her social standing, which would usually take a dive after turning down such an eligible proposal, soared. And, of course, Clem and Lucinda still had their little tea-time jewellery conferences, while Clem flirted harmlessly and Lucinda stroked his ego and they giggled at each other and Ida brought them ices and sweets and tried not to be –

Was that next word going to be 'jealous,' Ida Finn? Seriously? She really needed to sort out this Clem situation. At some point. But, before anything else, there was a little something she needed to take care of. Reggie Powell was out on a date.

He'd happened to buy a sweet little necklace from a certain strawberry-blond salesman, and the information of their little rendezvous had leaked back to The Rat Prince. Shame, that.

They were walking along the river. Well, that was the intention. The two seemed to get distracted every few steps by each other's mouths. Little Peggy Coe from the Lord and Horse was attractive, Ida had to admit – in a cute, innocent, slightly dim way. Like a puppy.

The pair giggled at each other, and then the girl took Reggie by the hand and led him, still giggling, into a darkened alleyway, lit only by an old, flickering lamp.

Perfect.

Reggie Powell's legs looked like were about to give way underneath him. The girl of his dreams had finally – finally! – agreed to step out with him for an evening. And here she was, pressed up against him, his necklace at her pretty, dusky throat, her lips so soft, her hands gently stroking the nape of his neck, her eyes shining up into his when they finally broke apart, and when she parted her lips to whisper his name, so sweetly…

'Reegg…'

The iron-on-stone rasp behind him made Reggie shriek. He almost leapt into Peggy's arms as The Rat Prince leered down from the top of the lamppost at the end of the alleyway. There was something new in his voice; a growl, filled with quiet, devastating fury that sounded almost demonic.

'"The brooch was a gift", you said… you lied to me, Reg…'

'No…no…my mam just didn't want it,' Reggie spluttered, stepping in a puddle as he backed away, his face a mask of fear, his ankles soaked. 'It wasn't her colour. It wasn't her colour!'

Slowly, ever so slowly, The Rat Prince drew a shining silver blade from his belt.

'No one ever lies to me, Reg…'

Ida hoped that little Peggy Coe could look after herself in a genuinely dangerous situation, because if Reggie Powell had ran out of that alley any faster, he would have hurled himself straight into the river Lox. The young girl looked up at her potential attacker, pouting ferociously. She stamped her foot once, with enough force to send a shockwave through Loxport, and then stormed off after her beau, screaming his name along with every unladylike insult under the sun.

Ida laughed happily as she dangled one-handed from the lamppost like a monkey in a menagerie. The Rat Prince really is the bane of Loxport, she thought, as she dropped to the ground, vaulted the alley's brick wall, and melted away into the night. And I'm not going anywhere.

Epilogue

―――――

The boy stands alone in the green city, Barefoot and afraid. He has nothing. Is nothing, has never been, will never be. Above, raptors cry, swoop down, tear skin, rip his clothes from his back.

'Arrogant, ignorant boy. You think you can hide from who you are? Your hidden accent, your poor schooling, with your simpers and smiles. A wretched soul, lost and alone. That is all you are. All you can be.'

The birds whisper in a faintly familiar voice

'Tread lightly, boy. That wonderous, rebellious mind shall drown us all one day. Soon.

Soon.'

Clem's back was slick with sweat as he tossed and turned beneath the sheets. He awoke as if he'd been dragged to the surface of a pitch-black lake. He lay there for a moment, his heart stuttering in his chest. He never had nightmares; at least, not like this. When he did, it was about simple, easily forgotten things. Things he could brush aside. Missing a deadline for a commission, seeing an ex-lover in the street. And, recently, about Ida in shackles. But these new dreams were new.

He got out of bed and splashed his face with water

from the tiny porcelain sink. His bedroom was above the smithy. It comforted him to know that everything he needed was in one place. His little cave of wonders.

The Kaelinite sat on his workbench downstairs, ready to be used. Ida was coming around tomorrow, with Edith. He'd somehow found himself a whole group of friends, without really trying. Which was new, for him. He had so much to show them, so many new plans for the Kaelinite, and what they could do with it. What he could do with it. How he could control it. His mind was brimming with thoughts, leaping around his head like sparks.

He'd tasted the Kaelinite's powers when he'd originally owned the gem, before all this began, and the memory of the dreams he'd seen made him shudder. But now he was ready. His little white lie to his friends would be forgotten when he showed them what he could do. Whatever the Kaelinite was going to throw at him, he could handle it.

City of darkness. City in fear. Rats scurry in plain sight.

Slyly judging eyes, mocking laughter, bright as fire. None can hide. Pink flowers turn to viper's nests, slick red with bloodied lips. Teeth graze skin, and all around is laughter. Laughing at you.

Light will cleanse. Light will stop the laughter. Let there be light.

Lord Devon Casterbury woke from a most peculiar dream. His heart was racing uncomfortably hard, and his hair was plastered to his forehead. Damnably strange.

He swung his legs out from underneath the silk sheets

and padded through his house. His servants had long since gone to bed, though he could wake them with a short, sharp bellow and watch them scramble to make him a cup of tea. But, no, he knew what would calm his nerves.

Lord Devon Casterbury's house was full of beautiful things; elegant furniture, beautiful paintings, rare blueprints for famous inventions framed and polished every day as if they were his own. But, in the dark, two things glittered.

One is his engagement ring for Lucinda. He left it in its box, open, so that the light from his other treasure was trapped inside it.

Other men would have sold the ring after being refused, or demanded a refund. Lord Devon Casterbury had kept it. It was his property, after all, and he was sure it would come in useful again, sooner or later. But tonight, it was not his goal.

The Sentinel still shone its emerald light across the hallway, just inside the front door, untouched on that wretched evening six weeks ago. It still worked, but the light inside the gem was fading. It would have to be replaced soon. Lord Devon Casterbury wandered over to it and stared into the glow until his eyes swam with a multitude of colours as he blinked. His heart finally stilled; he was safe. No one could get in.

Not through the front door, anyway.

But he hadn't come through the front door, had he? No.

Lord Devon Casterbury lit the gas lamp in his study and scrawled out a note. He needed answers. His contacts had told him they had discovered a seam of

Kaelinite over a fortnight ago – where were they with his delivery? He'd funded the expedition; it was his boat. Brand new and beautiful. The Brilliance. He demanded to see results within the week, or he would… well, he wasn't sure what he'd do.

That Kaelinite was going to save Loxport. Save him. The city needed Sentinels, and much more besides. He needed it. Once it was here, no one would ever embarrass Lord Devon Casterbury again. He had plans, he had patents in place, he had freelance inventors waiting for his missive that their materials had finally arrived, that production could begin. And then they'd see what was what.

Casterbury signed his note with a flourish, fished a bottle of brandy out from the drawer next to his desk and took it back to bed with him. Trapped within the brandy's warm copper colour was a sickly green glow from the Kaelinite, stretching out its tendrils as he drank.

Thanks for reading *Clockwork Magpies*, if you enjoyed the book please consider leaving a review.

Acknowledgements

——

Thank you so much to Vic Watson and my fellow Elementary Writers, who heard Ida's story long before anyone else, and for your endless support as Loxport grew over the years. Thank you to the judges and readers of the 2020 *Times / Chicken House Children's Fiction Competition*, and to Northodox Press – you saw potential in a quirky little YA story from Up North, and I'm forever grateful.

Thank you to all the amazing booksellers I've had the pleasure of working with over the years– for all the hysterical laughter, the hot drinks, the teary hugs and sweary rants, and the wonderful book nerd chats. If you don't know a bookseller, readers, find one and make friends with them. They are   literally magic.

Thank you to my mam for reading the first draft, for all the 'homework notes', and for being proud of me when I couldn't be proud of myself.

Thank you to Harley, for always being Devon Casterbury's number one fan.

Thank you to Nina, for keeping me company on the

sofa as this book took shape during lockdown. And thank you to you, my readers. Whether you're a prickly, socially anxious mess like Ida, feel your feelings a little too strongly like Edith or talk too much like Clem; these characters are little pieces of my heart. And, just as much, they're for you.

NORTHODOX
PRESS

HOME OF NORTHERN VOICES

 FACEBOOK.COM/NORTHODOXPRESS

 TWITER.COM/NORTHODOXPRESS

 INSTAGRAM.COM/NORTHODOXPRESS

 NORTHODOX.CO.UK

SUBMISSIONS
ARE OPEN!
WRITER &
DEBUT AUTHOR
[ ]
NOVELS &
SHORT FICTION
[ ]
FROM OR LIVING
IN THE NORTH
[ ]

LOTTE JEAN ELLIOTT
THE
MONSTERS
CLUB
POPULARITY MEET PANDEMONIUM

THE GIRL
BENEATH
THE ICE

Lightning Source UK Ltd.
Milton Keynes UK
UKHW012246120223
416670UK00003B/38